Mark Sullivan is Mancunian from his Poundland socks to his five pound haircut. By day he answers the phone in a call centre, by night he sleeps with the fishes. This is his first novel, he is currently at work on his next book, *Friendly Kid*.

Corned Beef Sandwich

Mark Sullivan

This novel won the Crocus North West Novel Competition in 2001, judged by Elizabeth Baines, Phil Caveney and Qaisra Shahraz.

First published in 2002 by Crocus
Crocus books are published by Commonword Ltd, Cheetwood House, 6Mount Street, Manchester M2 5NS.

Commonword gratefully acknowledges financial assistance from the Association of Greater Manchester Authorities, Manchester City Council and North West Arts Board.

Crocus Books are distributed by Turnaround Publisher Services Ltd, Unit 3, Olympia Trading Estate, Coburg Road, Wood Green, London N22 6TZ.

Cover design by Ian Bobb.

Printed by MFP Print and Design, Unit E3 Langford Trading Estate, Thomas Street, Stretford M32 0JT.

British Library Cataloguing-in-Publication Data. A catalogue record for this book is available from British Library.

To Constable Beanland for services rendered.

One

Bang. You know how these things happen. It's the end of the day. You've just finished recounting the coppers to make sure you've got it right. Bagging up the money, rolling up the notes, making a record of how much we've made today, how much we've lost. When it strikes you. The sheer horrible beauty of life. How much you want to carry on living despite everything. Despite all the losing and getting nowhere.

In truth there haven't been many winners today. A couple of 10-1 shots in the 3:10 from Pontefract. The Capford Twins. They come in and bet the same amount on the same horse in the same race. I've asked them if they wanted me to put it through as a single bet, but they don't seem to get it. They look at me all despondent. They look at me like I'm the one that's slightly strange. Nose ring, eyebrow ring, another ring hidden from view, red hair, dressed in black, occasional deathblack eyeshadow. They have a point but it's more a question of situation. In the right situation you wouldn't give me a second look. That situation is probably the moshpit of a Marilyn Manson gig. This situation is a rundown prole bookies in south central Manchester.

So yes, Mr and Mr Capford Twin with your badly shaved heads, unwashed polo shirts and nose dribble, you have a point. It's a situation I intend to deal with. This is only temporary; this has only been temporary for the past year and a half. Plus the fact I like it. I like the sense of danger when a nice man in piss-stained dungarees threatens to rip out your gizzard for not putting his bet through on time. The sense of life's wonder and splendour when the Capford Twins try and kiss you though the glass as they celebrate their £26.42 win. Someone'll have to clean the goss off the glass later, but it's understandable in the heat of the moment.

We did have a couple of big losers today. One big big loser. And Charlie Strange had inside information. He told everyone in the shop, real horse's mouth natter. Flashing his money like it was his proud new penis extension.

'Where you got that?' Capford One wanted to know.

'Borrow it,' goes Capford Two. 'He borrow it.'

'Gonna win,' said Charlie Strange as happy as a man that's already won enough money to buy himself a new set of teeth to replace the ones he had knocked out of his face only three weeks ago. Plus he's got one of those fantastically romantic Action Man style scars down one cheek. And you have to say it suits him. For a man with no teeth, a still freshly scabbed cut down the side of his face, wearing spanking new white trainers, a three-piece accountant suit with no shirt underneath, gold rope chain and hair sculpted into a bizarre antigravity Elvis quiff - you have to say Charlie Strange is looking good. The fact that he has skin the colour of brown sugar fudge, a body that's strong like an earthquake, and green eyes that drill into you like a Black and Decker soul invader helps.

In fact if he was just a pair of eyes on a stick he'd do for me, but then I'm just an old romantic.

'Two hundred on the nose,' he said. Then there's the accent. The sort of Irish voice that makes fully grown paratroopers weep with fear. If it's possible to have a voice that sounds like an iron fist in a green mock velvet glove, Charlie Strange has. 'Two hundred on the nose.' Those were his exact words.

No betting slip. He gets me to fill them out for him. It's not a service we offer normally but he can't read and write either, so I'm his Slip Slave. His Betting Bitch my maladjusted brother called me when I tried to explain. Theo Short Pants, Charlie Strange called my brother the one time he popped into the shop to have a laugh and gawp at me. Then introduced himself to Charlie Strange like the arrogant fool he is. I told him, no one in here's gonna be impressed by your celtic thigh tattoos.

'Which horse?' I made a laugh sound like it was me that was simple. 'Which race?'

'On the nose.'

'Which horse?'

'On the nose.'

I wanted to ask again but he's got eyes like the devil when he's annoyed and the fire was starting to burn.

'Been told the name of the horse.' Charlie Strange looked like he was holding himself back; he closed his eyes and waited while his brain did some ticking. Behind him the Desponds had started queuing. There are about thirteen regulars. The voices muttering. The accents, the Bangladeshi, the Turkish, the Scottish, the Jamaican, the Irish, the Clampetts. The shop's like a social club for the local retired and terminally underemployed. All men in their fifties and sixties spending the day shooting the shit and taking advantage of the electric convector heaters and the unlimited collection of sawn-off biros, blunt stubby pencils and the cheap vend coffee machine. They could make all their 50p bets in one go at about ten past eleven in the morning when they arrive but that'd spoil their fun presumably. They like to wait till the last possible moment. Get me to make a mistake so they can get their money back when the bet gets void. They all know they're not going to win. They bet like other men fish. It passes the time; it makes them feel at one with nature. Not nature in the green fields, hello flowers, hello trees pastoral sense, more nature in the dog eat dog, chaos theory, sucked into a black hole of addiction sense.

Meanwhile Charlie Strange is explaining, 'It's a tip, do you see? Very good fella I know gives it to me. That's all there is to it. S'all I can say. He tells me he knows the jockey of a horse. Of a different horse to the one I'm betting on but he tells me he's very good. He says. The horse.'

'Okay.'

'So don't be asking me what race because I don't know. It's all new information to me. Straight from a friend of a jockey's mouth.'

If it was colder in here. If the electric convector heaters weren't turned up so bloody high there'd be steam coming out of Charlie Strange's flared nostrils. He's like a wild stallion that just needs taming and whispering to. I'm able to think - sitting behind an inch thick sheet of bulletproof glass. Though I'm not sure anyone has ever tested it to make sure. Though it does withstand hammer attack - or it did the last time someone tried.

'On the nose.' He pushed an elastic band wrapped bundle of notes through to me.

'Of which horse?'

'Is the name of the horse.'

'Oh.'

'Don't know what race it's in.'

'I'll have a look for you.'

They do this all the time. Race horse owners. For their own amusement probably, to annoy me more likely. Sit around in their mansion houses deciding what to call their new geegees. Names like Brian, Trevor or Lorraine get instantly rejected. For some reason Polly Golightly, Gay Challenger, Magik Babe, Mucky Jim, Gay Lover and Lady Boxer get accepted. It passes the time, gives them something to do when the horse is having its oats. Except some of the owners have to prove how clever they are. Come up with names like On The Nose, Some Horse, Give Us A Kiss, Another Horse and The Won Wot Wun.

So I had a look through the runners and riders and found the race starring the mighty gelding On The Nose. Counted out Charlie Strange's roll of notes. £205. He kept a fiver to buy him and his Capford Twin friends some chips and gravy. £200 On The Nose. Filled in the slip. 16-1. The horse came fourth. Charlie Strange took it quite well seeing as that is by far the most money he has ever held in his hand or had hidden down his jockey shorts. He didn't break anything. Harry my boss was very surprised. He expected trouble. Charlie Strange just sat slumped in the corner, then rolled up in a ball and started wailing, biting his nails and dribbling on the lino. I wanted to go out there and comfort him, but I didn't want him to blame me and start screaming and telling me he was going to kill me and all my dependants, which has happened before. But from an eighty-year-old incontinent it's not as frightening as it would be from Charlie Strange.

Besides, he disappeared eventually and the Desponds kept the 50ps rolling in. Then came the big one. Two big bets in one day, it's almost enough to keep us in business. In fact this one was more than enough. £3000. Someone I'd never seen before. Harry said he knew the type but it wasn't a type I'd ever seen before. Hey Big Spenders usually fit a pattern.

First there's the Social Spenders. They like to show off to their mates about how brave and rich and stupid they are. Then there's Secret Spenders. They're all furtive looks and three-day stubble. Need to bet to pay off their gambling debts. Convinced this is the big one. If you're a Social Spender it's not so bad; part of the point is that you're proving you can afford to lose. Lose easy, lose cool, win big, spend big. It's a nice philosophy. It would be nice to have the money to waste. Secret Spenders usually save enough money for a new pack of razor blades. Or go shoplifting for rope on their way home.

Funnily enough we don't get many old people betting big. Seems the old people round here prefer to spend their pension money on dog food and bleach. Apart from the Desponds, but I won't be drawn into criticising them. They pay my wages. Their loss is my £4.10 an hour.

Today's real Hey Big Spender was Welsh from what I could gather from the few words he spoke. Looked like a painting and decorating Clint Eastwood. Forties, short legs, moustache, blue paint speckled hair, acne pitted face making him look like he'd been attacked by a peddle-dashed wall earlier in his life.

Razor creased white tracksuit and vee of chest hair, flip-flops and sunglasses. Passes over the yellow slip before the money. Cheese Hamper 3-1 on. Simple enough. 4:20 at Goodwood, heavily fancied, likes it in the rain. Or so the Capford Twins were telling me. All well and good. £3000. Is an amount I'm not used to seeing scribbled in blunt pencil. Mr H. Big Spender pushing the noteage through the gap to back up the paper promise.

It takes you a moment to tally up this kind of happening. You have to take it in silently, make sure you don't show your shock. Or that's what I think if only cos the punters like it when you're shocked. Adds to the Social Spender thing. You're just someone else to show off to. Even if they do think you're a muppet with a Miss Piggy nose ring. They're like rich flashers. Except their wallets are bigger than their genitals.

'Harry, can you have a look at this for me?'

If we've got a bet this big I don't have the authority to accept it. That's Harry my boss's job. You don't do a job like this to accept responsibility. You get to age twenty-six and you're working as a betting shop counter assistant for precisely the opposite reason. You want to avoid making decisions; you want to carry on thinking big thoughts about your big dreams that are going to turn to gold reality any day now. Or dust if you're feeling worthless and realistic. So we take the bet. Mr H.B. Spender exits the shop with his slip tucked in his zipped up pants pocket. We watch the race with crossed fingers and legs. The Capford Twins get excited.

'Be gonna win,' says Capford One.

'Wet,' says Capford Two. 'Horse not like wet.'

'Horse like a fish,' says Capford One.

They go on blah blah horsey blah.

The horse runs hard, the commentator gets hoarse. Bracey Butter wins at 5-2.

'So, Harry, what's the chance of me getting a bonus?'

Harry looks at me with his boss face.

'I took the bet after all. Surely I deserve a bonus? That's three thousand quid - pure profit.'

Hermit Harry is stonefaced. He's too busy pushing his glasses up his nose, scratching his slaphead and picking his nose and chewing his crows to have any interest in anything I might want to say.

'What about a bit of that performance related pay stuff. Isn't it about time we had an employee share buying scheme where you buy shares for me type of thing?'

Harry huffed and wandered back to his office to do his so-called paper work.

So it gets to the end of the day. A good day. Leaving me yawning, wondering what I'll have for tea then remembering how I went over to Abdul's micro-mini-mart across the road about twoish. How I bought myself a halal corned beef sandwich but never got round to eating it. Got distracted by Charlie Strange, two packets of cheese'n'rotten crisps and a white chocolate Twix. So there's tonight's worry and tribulation taken care of. A culinary delight is in the offing. Toasted halal corned beef sandwich with a cup-a-soup chaser. And a sprig of parsley because parsley's nice and it's the only thing I've got in the fridge. Theo says it won't grow if I keep it in the fridge. He says I have to water it, it needs sunlight and warmth. But I want to keep it fresh. I don't want it going off.

So I put my sandwich in a brown canvas moneybag and shove the rest of my things in with it, keys, Maltesers, chewie, lip balm, deathblack eyeshadow, orange stick. I'd carry a little rucksack or shoulder bag but I'm not a shoulder-bag/handbag sort of person. They tend to fall off your wrist when you're in the moshpit at a Marilyn Manson gig. But I throw everything in and have a quick tidy round in the hope I might be able to knock off early for a change.

Harry's locking up. 'Don't mind cashing up tonight, do you, Harry? Only I've got to get home to feed my fish before half past. Or. Or they won't be happy.' I've got to get home. To watch telly and wonder why I never go out. To end up poking at the blackheads round my nose and end up looking such a mess I'll never be able to go out for about a week and a half because I'm all scarred.

'Can't do tonight, I'm afraid, Sunshine. Just had a call from the security people. Running fifteen minutes late. Apparently they've got traffic on the roads tonight.'

'Traffic on the roads?' As opposed to diseased geese on the roads wandering like shell-shocked Vietnamese war refugees. Now that's an excuse I wouldn't mind them offering. It's a geese issue. Sorry we're ten minutes late. We tried to tell Mother Goose but she just kept going on about the horror the horror and rubbing the top of her head with her wing. Still, we managed to shoo them into a lay-by and here we are, so there's no harm done, hey?

'Ah but, Harry?'

'Ah but nothing, Sunshine. We're both of us need to stay until the money's collected. You know company policy.' His voice up and down like an opera singer. An opera singer that smokes 50 a day.

'That's not what you normally say, Harry.'

'Sure and for normal we'd not have a total of almost four thousand nicker waiting to be collected. Hughie Jones wouldn't like it.'

'Yeah, yeah.' Hughie Jones is the owner, Harry goes on about him all the time. About what great friends they are. I've never seen him. He owns a chain of bookies in the South Central part of town and probably elsewhere, I don't really know. I'm not even sure he exists. Hughie Jones Turf Accountants is probably just a loveable name to make the shop seem more homely. Otherwise we'd be called Steal From The Poor Bookies or Betting Is For Idiots. 'Even so,' I start whining, 'couldn't you just let me go early this once?'

'No chance of that t'night. Or do you not think ...'

'What?'

'Oh nothing. You get on with the counting, Sunshine.'

'Alright. I'm counting aren't I?'

I'm counting money as carefully as Mr Scrooge. Except none of it belongs to me and if I knew a little Cratchett boy with spindly legs who really needed a turkey I'd buy him one. To keep as a pet, mind. I don't eat anything that's intelligent enough to fly or swim. Pigs and sheep I have no qualms about slaughtering. Cows have a big eyelash model girl look that annoys me so they get the chop. Hens and their tastier younger chicken sisters I'm in two minds about. They fly about as well as I do. Though if you're sat in a metal cage all day you're never going to learn, so the jury's out.

'Harry, do we accept Irish money?'

'In theory no. In practise it depends how much they're betting and whether I'm due to go and visit my mammy.'

Harry's going through the books. I don't know what he does but he sits in the office smoking and looking over his glasses at sheets of paper with numbers on them. That's probably all he is doing because I don't think he understands all this turf accounting nonsense.

'Harry, do we accept Monopoly money?'

'In theory no. In practise it depends how big the fella is.'

I've finished counting. I've finished re-counting. The money's in a bag ready to go.

'Harry?'

'No Bulgarian money. No buttons, money off tokens, wage slips or fake gold watches.'

'Harry?'

'Yes?'

'What do I do when someone's pointing a gun at me through the glass?'

'The glass is bullet-proof, Sunshine, you've nothing to worry about.'

The glass is over an inch thick and very strong. My skin if penetrated by a bullet is paper thin and very soft thanks to years of Vaseline Intensive Care and Oil of Olay rubbed into the elbows.

'Harry?'

'What is it now?'

'Harry please.'

It must be something in my voice. A note of horror, alarm, fear, anguish. Or perhaps he can smell the fact that I am rapidly wetting my pants. As if from nowhere, like a genie out of a magic lamp, or a ski-masked armed robber from an unsupervised gent's toilet, stands a silent man with a revolver. He's not saying anything. He's not doing anything. Or I should say, he's not doing anything else apart from pointing his gun directly at my face. I'm protected by inch thick bullet-proof glass but at this very instant my faith in a bunch of workshy glaziers from Warrington is perhaps not total.

'What d'you want?' Harry asks the masked invader.

There doesn't seem much doubt in my mind what he wants. He just can't bring himself to ask. He's too polite. Or he doesn't want us to recognise his voice.

The gun stays steady. Stays pointed at my face. There's a click like a piece of machinery moving into place.

'We don't want any trouble,' says Harry. Me and Mr Gunman locked in a staring contest with the sound turned down. His piercing green eyes staring at me like Kryptonite laser beams.

'I think we better do as he says,' says Harry inching up by my side. I don't want to move, I don't want to make a wrong move. 'You know we have cctv cameras here, don't you?' says Harry. 'You'll not get away with this.'

Of course Harry forgets to say that the cameras haven't worked for about a month and Hughie Jones hasn't been arsed to send an engineer round to fix them yet. 'We're not going to try any funny business so you needn't get worried, Sir.' He calls the robber, *'Sir.'* Like he's visiting royalty. That annoys me. I like an armed robber who defers to me. Gives me a bit of respect despite the fact that he's destroying my confidence and taking everything I've got. 'I'll pass you through this bag. That's all our takings for today. Then I'll come out there and open the door for yous. We don't want any trouble.'

Harry seems to think that this isn't actually *any trouble*. Whereas I'm sort of thinking this is the most trouble I have ever experienced in my life. Harry squishes the moneybag through the slot where I take the 50ps, pay out the £1.71 winnings to the Desponds. The gunman nods and takes the bag in his left hand, lowers the gun and waits for Harry to come through and let him out. He looks at me one more time and I don't know if he's smiling behind his ski-mask but he should be. Harry opens the door to the shop and the gunman runs off in his squeaky clean white trainers.

'Harry,' I say.

'I know, I know,' he says. 'We have to call the Old Bill.'

'But Harry.'

'What?'

And I'm about to say something. I'm about to say it for about three tenths of a second then it's like I'm at the dentist and he's sprayed freezing cold foam into my mouth so it won't move. It's the devil's dentist that often visits me in dreams, not Mr Crumbshaw who umms and ahhhs and tells me I need another filling in my lower third molar.

'That was.'

'A terrible experience.'

'Do you know.'

'What it's like to have a gun pointed at your head? No, and it's not a feeling I want to know about either.'

'But I think I know who.'

'Is to blame for all this violence. It's the government whichever way you look at it. They should bring back hanging and birching. That must seem a funny thing to talk about right now but if I could get my hands on that big bugger I'd wring his bloody neck I would.'

'Harry?'

'Have we called the po-lice?'

'No, Harry.'

'And call yourself a cab why don't you, while you're at it. I'm not having you walking home on a night like this. Why you must be all shaken up.'

'Shouldn't I ... don't I have to stay for the police?'

'In the state you're in? Why, you're a bag of nerves, aren't you not? What, get yourself home and get your feet up, get a few drinks inside you. They've got me to ask questions. I was here, was I not? Oh and Sunshine, when you've made your calls, will you put the kettle on for us? That'd be grand if you did. I know I'll be waiting me arse off for these police fellas to turn up. Take for ages they always do. Can talk to you in the morning can they not? As good then as it is now. Experience like this, it's not the sort of thing you're gonna forget in a hurry, is it?'

I'm too shaken to argue. It happened so quickly. I need to press reverse rewind and replay in my head. I'm in a daze as I call 999 then Ab's Cabs and tell the people on the other end where I am and tell them it's an emergency.

The taxi comes first and Harry tells me to get

myself off home, so I grab my bag with my keys and my sandwich inside and go and sit in the back of the car. The driver's busy talking with Abdul from across the road about what's been going on. Then we're speeding away ultra-fast in the big black car like I'm escaping royalty. Escaping from a bunch of Kings and Duchesses who are giving chase on motorised scooters. Is the way I like to think about it.

So I try to just concentrate on looking out of the window at all the ignorant people wandering about. All so ignorant of the pain and sorrow I'm suffering. Do my relaxation exercises; breathing in and out. In and out. In, out, resisting the urge to shake it all about. I try and breathe deeply from the stomach as I pull open the neck of the brown canvas bag and reach in for my lip balm. At times like this you need all the protection you can get. Except. There is no lip balm in this bag. And no halal corned beef sandwich.

Two

And no halal corned beef sandwich. It takes a moment to sink in. Then another moment and I'm home and it's time to pay the taxi driver. My money was in the other bag with my lip balm and keys and whatever else it was that I've lost forever.

'I...' I start. 'I think I've.' I'm full of half sentences today. 'Is it okay if I pay you...' I'm looking in the bag. The thought that comes to mind is: with a fifty pound note.

'You've been through a lot, yeah?' says the taxi driver, nodding his head to the music, revving the engine. 'Pay me tomorra. Sort it out tommora. Pay our Abdul, yeah? He knows what's goin on.'

'Cheers,' I'm nodding and holding the moneybag like a mother with a first baby. Holding it so tight I'm strangling it.

'Take it easy, yeah.'

And I'm floating out of the car without really realising it. Standing in front of the house I share with Theo, Sheena and Axel.

It's a fifteen-minute walk to work. I don't have to be there till 10:30ish. It's an ideal job in many ways. The pay isn't great, the hours are good. I've lost my door keys, and I'm standing in the rain strangling a bag full of almost £4000 in coins and notes. I should know. I counted it myself. Twice. And it weighs considerably more than lip-balm and a sandwich. You'd have to be in shock not to notice. But. But I can discuss this with myself later.

I live in the sort of area where if you go out after dark you'll get mugged before you get out of your front garden. Or that's what I tell people when I'm trying to impress them. That's what I tell myself when I'm thinking up excuses as to why I never leave the house. So the thing to do now is to get inside as quickly as possible.

I break into a sudden run and bound my way through the gate and up the path, weave past the wheely bin and I'm on the step and hammering at the door. Sweating and panting like I've just been robbed. Then I remember we've got a doorbell so I ring that instead. Someone will be in.

I have a look through the letterbox. Axel padding down the stairs in his bare feet, surf shorts, bare chest, and hair band.

'Okay okay.'

I'm still pounding and rapping the letterbox knocker. I've got a force in me I can't control. I've got something to tell everyone.

Then Axel swings open the door and his face is a stoner-weightlifter grimace of pissed-off-ness. Like hey, he was taking a joint break here. He don't want to be disturbed. He's gotta get back down into the cellar in a minute and pump some more iron.

'So what's your problem, huh?' goes Axel. Not that pissed off actually. But then he's from California like he's always telling us. He lived there till he was eight. So he's pretty chilled on the surface. Devious, narky and whining underneath his blonde surf god exterior. 'Rain huh? Shit. This weather does not agree with me.' And he starts wandering off, smoking his blunt, loping down the hall towards the cellar door. So he can blast us all with Tupac Shakur and wank his body up to size.

'Axel. Wait, Axel.'

'Yeah? What's occurring?'

'I've just been robbed.'

I've got to get it off my chest. I can't keep it to myself.

'No shit? I tell ya. These streets? The minute I get my shit together and get some cash money in my pocket? I'm gonna get myself down the store and buy me some protection.'

'He had a gun.'

'That's what I'm sayin. Need somethin light that'll fit in your jacket. Something tasty for the homelife. Something that packs a punch for the mo's that's comin through the windows.'

'You can't buy guns in a shop can you?'

'Get a licence ya buy what ya want. But I aint talkin Woolworths here,' he's started so he'll finish. It's me with the story to tell, I'm the one that had the reality-bites-excitement. I'm the one that had the pant-wetting experience. Instead I'm standing in the hall getting my breath back listening to him wheedle on about his shady gangster contacts, the size of the weapons he's going to buy etc etc etc. 'We are talking strictly for the underground here. You know someone, someone know someone else, piece is on the table before breakfast. Like a toy that just fallen outta your corn pops. That's the truth.'

'Okay. I better let you get on,' I say. Meaning. Fuck off, Axel, you're full of shit and we both know it. I only put up with you because your rich daddy bought you this place and the rent's quite cheap.

See that's what Axel does. He's twenty-four, university drop out. Truth is he did well to drop-in in the first place. He's never read a book in his life. But apparently being able to read is not a big consideration these days. Certainly not if you're a part-time computer geek like Axel is. Part-time, retired. Which is how my little brother Theo knows him. Theo was doing the same thing at college, but lasted the course, got himself a supergeek job doing something with computers that has something to do with the Internet for some big company on the other side of town. Theo and Axel are wanting to go into business together. Axel owns this place, Theo wants to put money together and buy up shed loads of other places. Convert them into flats for reprobates, desponds, lifetime losers, single parents and students. It's where the money is these days apparently. Poverty.

But at least with Axel being such a self-centred dope-addled fantasy life twat there is no danger that he might draw out my secrets.

So I rush up to my room on the top floor. Thinking. Why am I being so secretive, why am I talking about secrets? Because I've got a canvas bag packed with about £4000 under my arm.

A mistake an honest lucky mistake.

I'm going to give it back.

Trying to open my door. Realising that, of course, it's locked. I'm locked out of my own room. My fish are starving; they've not been fed since yesterday. Little baby Kurt Kobain, Tankgirl, Lorraine, Judas and Satan'll start eating each other. They'll be pining for my company. They miss me when I'm not there.

And I sit in the doorway to my room with my head in my hands and just start crying. In my mind is a memory of Charlie Strange buckled up into a foetal heap weeping at his loss. I'm £4000 richer and I feel just the same. It doesn't make any sense. I'll have to give it back and then I'll feel like I've lost £4000 and how bad will that feel. I'm confused and sobbing but then I remember I hid a spare key with my junk stuff in the cellar so I go downstairs to get it.

Try and pull myself together before I open the cellar door, get hit by a motherfuckin bitch whining wall of sound. The sight of Axel in his surf shorts straining like I only do when I'm especially constipated.

'Sorry,' I shout, 'just got to get something.' And I make my way over to the corner, to my pile of cardboard boxes full of plastic bags full of bricabrac and things I've bought off white elephant stalls at jumble sales. Or that's what it seems like. A contraption for doing sit-ups that I never sat up and did. Cleaning products for face, body, soul and bathroom that didn't agree with me for some reason but were too expensive to ever throw out. Bags of hippy and schoolyard clothes that seemed like a good idea at the time but are too embarrassing to hand into a charity shop, too sentimental value to go in the bin. A massive clear plastic bag full of asphyxiated cuddly toys that there is no earthly reason to keep. Garfield, Paddington Bear, Snoopy. A bag full of embarrassment waiting to happen. Underneath it all. Axel looking over like he thinks I've just made some dumb excuse to come down here and marvel at his bod. Then his mobile rings and he's got other things to think about. Underneath it all is an enormous pottery pig with a coin slot in its nose, an entry hole under its arse and a collection of holiday foreign coins inside. A penknife, some Christmas wrapping paper, some Christmas holly-and-ivy Sellotape, a spare front door key and a spare room key. That no one's supposed to know about, that I almost forgot about. Which just goes to prove that sometimes it does pay to be a compulsive-obsessive hoarder and just-in-case extra key cutter.

'You found what you lookin for?' says Axel walking his wide-legged walk over to me, phone still clamped to his ear. A *you wanna fuck me, don't you?* smile on his face as he looks down at me scratching around on my knees. Not in this lifetime, friend. But then he's probably only being friendly. I have to try and remember, make a mental note, not everyone is as insane as I am. Another phone goes off while he's still talking so he goes back over to answer it. It's a busy life he leads, sloping round the house picking things up and putting them back down.

Upstairs, scratchy new key resisting at first but going in when I push it. Inside my room. The bag of £4000 still sitting outside my door. As if it's just got a sandwich in. And I'm feeling as hungry as a goldfish that's not been fed for twenty-five hours.

First things first. Take care of those you love. I get down on my knees and sprinkle some flakes into the water for my babies. Tankgirl with her suckerfish face pressed against the glass, as usual not taking any notice of the excitement all around her. Judas, Lorraine and Satan coming over to dance in the corner for me like excitable Labradors. Stopping occasionally to pick up little stones and gargle with them then puke them back out when they realise they taste like polished rock.

Then they're coming to the top and eating. And I'm having to persuade timid little Kurt Kobain the silver-white fish of the family to join in and eat. He's so miserable and anti-social and anorexic. He reminds me of myself except thinner, more beautiful and a better swimmer. But baby Kurt if he could sing it wouldn't be worth hearing. It'd be a fish whine about the unfairness of tank life. But it's a sign of someone who spends too much time alone with their fish that I know what type of songs they would sing if they had voices and recording contracts.

I need to concentrate on what's going on around me. Someone's knocking on the door, little brother Theo.

'Hey, just been speaking to Axel? What's been goin on? Someone tried to shoot you in the street?'

'It was at work.'

'They didn't have a gun?'

'They had a gun.'

'That's what I heard.'

'You heard right then.'

'Hey, I'm only asking.'

'Well if you'll let me tell you.'

'Look I'm only tryin to help. Only tryin to show a bit of fuckin compassion. Why do we always have to fuckin argue like this? Come home from work. Speak to Axel. And that's the thanks I get.'

'Sibling rivalry,' I say trying to make a joke out of it. Theo was the one person five minutes ago I was going to tell. As much as a computer munching, money obsessed twat as he is, we are close. 'Listen, Theo, sorry to get all...'

'Yeah you're right. You should be sorry.'

So it turns into a someone-else-in-the-limelight-my-problems-in-the-margins conversation.

'Okay well, you're okay now?'

'Yeah, still a bit in a daze. It all seems... weird.'

'Bound to, bound to. Look I've gotta grab a shower I'm meeting Ava about five minutes ago.'

'Sure sure, don't let me stop you.'

'Right. If you need to... talk or whatever? Get me on my mobe. Probably stayin at Ava's tonight so catch you tomorrow morning if not before.'

'Right yeah. Good luck.'

'Good luck is one thing I don't need,' he says in his reassuringly obnoxious and arrogant way. I know where I'm going, he says. I know what I want out of life. I can make £4000 a week as a contract worker with my skill level. I can make £4000 overnight if I buy that house across the road and sell it as a flat share development opportunity.

Theo clicks the door shut behind him with a strange amount of care and consideration. A click that sounds like a revolver being cocked ready to shoot.

So I'm left lying on my back on the floor of my room. A glass tank full of stomach-full fish by my side, floorboards gently throbbing to the sound of the Notorious BIG. And a canvas bag full of notes, coins and the odd money off voucher behind my head. And the thought:

I've got the gunman's money.

He's got my lip balm, my keys, my corpse black eyeshadow, my halal corned beef sandwich.

The gunman has got the keys to my house.

I lie on my back and listen to the sound of Theo taking a shower; to Axel body-porking about in the cellar; to the front door opening and swinging shut. And I'm left with the thought:

The gunman has got the keys to my house.

Three

The gunman has got the keys to my house. And someone's coming in the door. Am I going to be shit scared every time the door opens and shuts? I inch open the door a slither and listen. Nothing. But then my gunman is known for the silent way he creeps up on people. Or the silent way he creeps up on me. Then the phone's ringing and there's a laugh that sounds like a witch cackling. It's okay, it's only Sheena. The last of my house people. Chatting on the phone while she unlocks the door to her room, on the ground floor at the front. And I'm standing out on the landing like the saddest person in the world trying to work out who she's talking to and what she's talking about. What she's just said about me in her annoyingly friendly Geordie accent.

'No, it was crackin. Absolutely.' This'll be her holiday no doubt. She's just back from an executive hop and stop island tour of Thailand. And don't we know about it. 'Gotta be careful over there mind. Aye, hot I'll tell yeh it's hot. Wait up, I'll just check, usually is around about at this time.'

Sheena shouts up the stairs to me with her foghorn voice at full volume. I wait as if I was busy doing something interesting in my room. Then lock my door and go down. And Sheena carries on gabbing to whoever it is wants to talk to me while I stand in the hall and watch. 'No the job's goin smashin. I tell yeh what, say what yeh like about my company and the environment people an all that, but the characters that work there are diamond.' Sheena does PR for a nuclear processing plant. Her short skirts and up-for-a-laugh style goes down crackin. Takes people's minds off the two headed fish and rivers that glow in the dark.

Not that I'm jealous, as Theo is always happy to remind me. 'And you're not jealous,' he says.

'I'm not,' I say.

'No you're not are you.'

'No. I'm not.'

So at least we agree on something. I'm not jealous of Sheena with her company car and her friends and her cropped peroxide blonde hair and so-tiny-you-can-hardly-notice-it diamond nose stud.

She witters on, I try not to listen, 'Aye and I'm promised a pay rise at the end of the month so everything's goin swimming.'

Sheena once had a thing with our Theo. But then Theo's had a thing with just about anybody you care to mention. To hear him when we're watching the local news he's had half the criminals and most of the presenters. There isn't a Pamela Anderson look-a-like in the city he hasn't had. To hear him. And whilst the reality might not be as gruesome as all that, he is strangely successful with the ladies for a thigh, waist and ankle tattooed computer freak.

I've never seen the attraction personally.

Or maybe I can see the attraction and just don't like it. It's like the big wheel, it's an attraction, you might like looking at it but you wouldn't necessarily want a ride. Too boring by half when you've got tickets for the rollercoaster is my way of looking at it.

But then Theo's my brother in the way the moon is related to the earth. They've hovered around together since the beginning of time or the invention of watches, but the earth's full of chalk and the moon's made of cheese.

His parents fostered and adopted me before he was born. They didn't think it was possible to have a child like Theo. Loud, obnoxious, whining, generally babyish. At least that was my opinion of the tiny little brat. But then I was only three so what did I know. Unlike most unexpected babies Theo wasn't a mistake; he was a miraculous surprise. Both the parents, all the relations, were overjoyed and grateful. And it's Mum now, on the end of the phone line gabbing away to Sheena. I roll my eyes hoping Sheena might get the message, but she's too busy being nice to my Mum. People always say how viper pleasant she is, but that's why she works in the snake-eat-mouse world of public relations. She gets people to like her then swallows them whole and spits out their gizzards. But then she has the natural advantage of being a Geordie and having people like her the moment she speaks. It's the same as being Irish when it comes to phone talk and impressing people. Except you wouldn't mind if you phoned up a sex line and there was an Irish voice on the other end. A Geordie voice and it just wouldn't work.

Aye that's canny. Dinna stop, pet, dinna stop.

Finally Sheena starts winding up and gives my Mum a last cheery goodbye before handing the receiver over to me. Her mobile's ringing in her bag.

'Hi Mum.'

'Hello Hon, and what have you got to tell me?'

'About what?'

'I was just having a nice little chat with that friend of yours, Sheena.'

'I know, I was waiting.'

33

'Telling me all about who she's been seeing, where she's been going. Did you know she's been on holiday to Thailand?'

'I had heard yes.'

'It sounds fascinating.'

'Doesn't it.'

'And she's getting promotion at work.'

'*Really?*'

'Buying new clothes.'

'All the time.'

'Doing all right for herself. Must have the boys flocking round.'

'Like dogs round a lamp post.'

'Sorry?'

'Hmm?'

'So how you coping, Hon? Had any thoughts about college?'

I refuse to answer this question. I let the silence hang.

'I was looking through some, what do you call them, brochures.'

'Mum, I don't do college.' I do designer drugs, kinky sex and the occasional spot of yoga. But I don't do getting taught. I failed my exams when I was at school for a purpose. I wanted out.

'They do all sorts of courses these days. Your Dad and I were having a look through some of the prospectuses on this website he was showing me. You can even do courses in hat-making these days.'

'No.'

'Pottery, Cultural Studies, which sounds interesting. Watching the telly that's what that's all about according to your Dad. I thought you might be interested.'

'Mum, you can either change the subject or I can put the phone down.'

'You know you really can be quite nasty some times.'

'Sorry.' Fact is Mum'd be happy if I did a course in sex tourism so long as it was a course and we could all share the illusion that my life was going somewhere.

'You should study politics, you'd be good at that. Lots of arguing.'

'Yeah.'

'So what have you been up to? Any luck on the job front?'

'We had an armed robbery today.'

'Sorry?'

'A man came in with a gun. Pointed the gun at my head.'

I miss out the inch of bulletproof glass bit. It spoils it somehow.

'No?'

'Yes.'

'I don't know what to say,' says my Mum who might not know *what* to say but she always has *something* to say. 'Do you want me to come round?'

'No, I'll be okay.'

'And are you alright? What do the police say? Have they caught him? Was there more than one? Did anyone get hurt? Did *you* get hurt? I'll get your father. I'm not having this, we'll come round and visit.'

'Mum, it's two hundred miles.'

Dad's wheeling up to the phone, Mum telling him about me working in *that* terrible place. Living in that house she doesn't like. In that area she doesn't want anything to do with. Blah blah gibber gabber blah.

'Mum, it's okay,' I say though no one's listening. 'Don't worry.'

'Hello? This is your Dad speaking,' he says just in case there's going to be any confusion. Hello, this is your Mum speaking through a tuba.

'Hello, Dad.'

'What's all this then?'

'What's all what?'

I could stretch this conversation out for another five minutes but eventually he'd end up shouting at me and I'd end up shouting back and Mum'd end up crying for the both of us.

'Dad, it's nothing to worry about, these things happen all the time.'

'Do they cobblers. If they happened all the time there'd be people dead all over the streets. I'm well aware of what life's like in an urban environment, but armed robbery's not normal and it's not to be encouraged.'

'Dad, I know.' I don't know when he started talking like this. I blame the Internet. American conspiracy theorists have poisoned his brain. But it does make life easier, it means I can argue with him about something meaningless and less personal than the lack of direction in my life. I'm scarcely even listening, I let him go on for a bit then cut in. 'Dad, you don't understand. You live in the countryside.'

Then Mum's back and really it makes you think there must be some advantages to being an orphan.

'Mum, it's okay. I'm a bit shaken up, but I'll be fine. I wish I'd never brought it up.'

'I'm glad you did. Something like this happens I want to know.'

'Look Mum, I think something's burning in the oven. A casserole.'

'Well at least you're eating.'

'Gotta go Mum.'

'Is Theo looking after you?'

'Yeah, course he is.'

'I hope so. Can I have a word with him?'

'He's gone out with this Ava.'

'*Who*? And left you after someone's being trying to *shoot* you? Left you to your own devices. Wait till I speak to that boy.'

'Alright then, better go.'

Sheena's in the kitchen when I go through to make a brew up. She's taken off her jacket now, wearing some sort of silky low-cut vest top, chopping vegetables and listening to bland FM. The top not quite low cut enough to show off her tit tattoo. A love heart on her left breast. Or so Theo and Axel tell everyone. And Sheena's happy enough to show it off. Apparently. After a couple of minutes of goading and daring. And a couple of extra vodka and limes into the bargain. Which is fair enough. The only problem I have with her tit tattoo is that love heart tit tattoos are so last year. But for Sheena it's next year, the year after, and every tit drooping year till she drops. Which will probably make for good conversation when she's dribbling into her bath in a care home.

'Couldn't help overhearing,' she says.

You could, you could try not listening, I don't

say.   'Sounded terrible what you were saying to your mam.'

'What about me gettin held up at gunpoint?'

'No, the way you were going on telling her you'd put the phone down if she ... Gunpoint?'

'Never mind. Forget it.' I fill and flick on the kettle. Forced to wait. 'S'not interesting.'

'No, go on.' She wants to be my friend. She hates me. She wants to be my friend, she hates me.

'Just an in-joke.'

'That I'm not in on?'

'No.' I don't care either way.

She huffs. If she wasn't such a strong character she'd burst into tears. Instead she'll go and tell tales to the landlord. Still jerking off his body in the cellar.

The phone rings again.

'I'll get it. Be Mum with some more advice for me.' I run and pick up the phone on the fourth ring. 'Hello? Mum?'

There's no one there. Or else. There is someone there but they're not saying anything.

'Hello?'

Nothing. Space silence seconds passing.

'Hello? Is there a problem on the line? Can you hear me? Knock once for yes, twice for no ... No. I'm hanging up now, goodbye.'

The phone gets hung up on the other end before I have chance. I 1471 but the electro-operator gives me the old, *'The caller has withheld their number,'* in her young Queen Mother voice.

'Who was that?' Sheena shouts through, still

slicing, dicing and munching her raw veg in the kitchen.

'Don't know. Wrong number.' I pick up a leaflet from next to the phone and order a pizza. It's not every day. I deserve to fill my face with cheese fat. It's not every day. I order a Hawaiian and this time don't get into a question and answer session with the phone boy about why ham and pineapple gets to call itself a Hawaiian pizza. Why green pepper and beef doesn't get to call itself a Russian pizza. He hasn't got the time, I haven't got the energy.

So I'm sitting on the stairs because Axel and Sheena are laughing and flirting in the kitchen for a change, and I don't want to be with my money in my room. My money. I don't want to look at it. Except the only money I had left was in my corned beef sandwich bag. So if I'm going to pay for this pizza I'm going to either have to borrow some money off Sheena. Which would make her very happy. Because I'd be in her debt. Or borrow a few pound from my bag upstairs. Which we'll call expenses. Which won't do any harm. Which isn't strictly speaking theft. Because I had my money stolen. And by the time I'm up on the second floor and emptying the contents of the money-bag onto the floor I've convinced myself. It won't do any harm. I'll return it later. Over in the tank Judas, Satan and Lorraine are dancing for me like the hungriest fish in the world. Little Kurt staring at me with his dark worried eyes and Tankgirl stuck on the side of the tank like someone's licked her and slapped her there. Stupid flat fish what does she know about money. Things just aren't as simple as you'd like them to be Kurt, I wish they were.

Then Axel's calling me cos my pizza's arrived like about as fast as if they've just microwaved it and delivered it by helicopter. Or else I've been standing staring at my money longer than I realised. I lock the door and go downstairs.

I've just had my first bad thought.

It's enough money to leave the country, it's just not enough to stay left.

'Got a guy on the phone wants to speak with ya,' says Axel, still in those shorts, now with an added sheen of sweat to his torso. Phone clamped to his ear as he nods at me coming down the stairs practising looking calm and unworried.

I go to the door and pay for the pizza with a twenty. I even give the lad a tip, which is the work of someone who definitely isn't me. I'm not a tipper; I'm an Ebeneezer Scrooge think-a-like who spends all day counting money.

'Standing by me this very sec,' says Axel with his eat-shit grin. 'The boy Theobald want to speak words with you.'

'Tell him I'm eating.'

'Says. Eating. Uh huh. Ya wanna invite your sib out for a drink huh? Hear that?'

'Tell him I've got no money.'

'Got no money. Thee say he know yous got money. Say ya hide it under your bed.'

'What? What you talkin about?'

There's no need for me to get worried. There's no need for my heart to beat this fast.

'Theo say ya got *enough* money.'

Do I have any money? I'm like someone who's lost a sandwich and found £4000. I don't know whether to laugh or cry or curl up in a ball and dribble on the carpet. In the meantime. 'I need to get this pizza eaten.'

'I'll help ya with that. No no,' Axel waving to me, 'wait up. Listen, Thee? Your sib gonna take some persuading. And you know what the lift situation is like. Like last time you all in my jeep? Look I don't care if the puke did wash off. Thee, I aint gonna take that chance.' He says to me, 'You drinkin tonight? I mean, are ya drinkin?'

'I shouldn't think so.'

'Okay. Thee, we're there in forty-five, alright? Hey, where's your baby Ava while this is all…? No shit. No shit. That's funny.'

And he's hanging up the phone.

And I'm still standing in the hall with my pizza box waiting for the king's permission to leave.

'Thee in BaaBaa. The one on the canal? His Ava she aint turning up tonight, no way, no how. He had her on the phone but now she aint even answering no text message. It's funny as shit when ya'll think how much that boy in love. Tell me he got a problem. Tell me Ava found out something he didn't want her to know. But I tell ya, when that boy say he got problems with a lady, you be sure he *really* got problems. The way I see it? The girl gone and she *aint* comin back.'

'I didn't know he was in love.'

'Ya didn't know? This was the one. Your boy Thee, he thinkin big time romance, all engagement rings an shit. Still, I gotta get fresh. You be ready in twenty, twenty-five?'

'I didn't say I was goin.'

'Oh yous goin. Thee say ya goin, you goin. He

tell me to take care of it.'

'My Mum said I was going, did she?'

'He did mention something about that come to think.' Axel smiles his honest onion smile and for a moment you could only love him. If he didn't carry on chatting shit and sweating. 'You aint going and I is in trouble with your Moms. And that aint a place I wanna be. So it's hook or crook, but yous comin. Alright?'

'Right now I'm eating. I'll let you know in fifteen minutes.'

'We leavin in twenty so get ready. Where's Sheena?'

I shake my head. I'm not interested. This is getting like a Christmas, New Year kind of situation. Members of my family telling me to cheer up, happy up, smile. Their every effort making me cringe and frown a little more. There is no hope for me really. People are only trying to help. I should lighten up, relax, not worry be happy.

Wrapped in a towel and dripping wet Axel comes into the tv room where I'm munching my Hawaiian style ham and pineapple pizza and watching MTV.

'Got a guy calling for ya. Irish dude.'

'Not on the phone again?' I ask him, chomping a last piece before I start up. Slipknot are on and I've got the sound up so loud I wouldn't be able to hear anything else.

'Nah, he's out on the stoop.'

I frown. An Irishman calling round to see me?

Axel exits and I've got a second or two to run through possible ideas. But the one that keeps coming back. The gunman's got my keys.

Wouldn't he just let himself in?

The gunman isn't gonna knock on the door and say hello.

Four

The gunman isn't gonna knock on the door and say hello. He isn't gonna say sir, madam, thank you kindly and please may I have. What'll happen is I'll give him everything I've got and if he wants he'll take the skin off my back as a bonus. Then he'll do something preposterous to my intestines as an interest payment, a handling charge.

I can laugh. I can make jokes.

I could if I was insane.

So luckily thanks to my insanity I'm not in the least bit scared to answer the door. And luckily social convention means I have no choice but to casually walk down the hallway eating the last bit of pizza and licking garlicky sauce off my fingers while my heart beats to a disco rhythm: dumb dumb dumb dumb.

Until I spot a familiar bald head and my heart leaps and I'm suddenly so happy that I might just momentarily float. My heart was in my mouth but now its poking its blue veins out of my ears. And then my heart sinks back down to my feet making them heavy. Footsteps slow as mud and painful as mermaids'.

It's Irish Harry my bookie boss.

So why is he here?

It's not the sort of thing he normally does: come round to sit on the hearth rug and chew the gristle with me. I'm not overly convinced he even likes me. But then he's so grumpy he might be in love with me for all I know. So I have to say, seeing him here, standing there on the doorstep: I'm mildly peeved, and peeved is not an emotion I normally do. It is not an emotion I have *ever* really understood, I do not know how to peeve or be peeved. Today, I'm superpeeved and I know exactly why he's round here. Or I think I do.

'Harry, what's happening?' I smile with a big cheese smile of relief that he isn't a masked man with a gun in his hand.

'Oooh I was just passin, y'know and I thought, I think I'll pop round an say hello.'

'That's nice.' I'm still munching.

Harry stands on the step, hands in pockets, 'So I've just bobbed round to check that you're feelin alright in yerself... How are yehs?'

'Oh, right yeah. Not too bad, fine, fine.' I smile, Harry frowns. Then I remember about the robbery thing. At least it seems like I'm remembering. It seems like I forgot for a millisecond. 'Y'know...' blah blah blah.

'Little bit shook up?'

'Little bit.'

I nod, Harry nods.

'Good. Good...'

I'm not gonna say anything if he's not. I don't know what I'm doing yet, I don't want Harry to decide for me.

'I see yeh treatin yeh self to a wee bit of that pizza. I myself can never afford to have those sorta takeaway items it seems, but then I'd rather have a cheese sandwich meself.'

'I'd offer you a slice but I'm...' Greedy. Unfriendly. Tight-arsed. You take your pick really.

'No, no, you're grand. You fill your chops, yeh deserve it. Now are you gonna invite me in or must I stand out here all the evening long?'

'Ha ha ha,' I laugh. But I'm not moving. He's not coming in no matter what he thinks. He's not my boss in this house.

That's Theo's job.

And Axel's job, obviously: in his role of penny-pinching landlord.

And Sheena's job. Because it just is.

And then there's little baby Kurt Kobain giving me all these orders and sarky remarks. Waffling on about my soul being in peril...

So I stand holding onto the door till my knuckles go white; pretending to be relaxed.

I have the body language of a badly controlled robot. I'm smiling but you'd have to be a robot to believe it.

'I've got a lot goin on actually, Harry. Just on my way out as it happens. Otherwise...' I'd have to make up some more complicated excuse to get rid of you.

'Well I won't keep you for long. Just a wee chat.' Harry steps forward and without punching him straight in the face I'm not left with much option. He is coming in. He walks past me and I step back, and now I'm standing outside. Like I'm the one that's just come visiting. Well at least this way he can't very well go and have a sit down on his own.

'It was a bad business today it was,' he says, scratching his sandpaper chin hair, his forehead crinkling and his eyebrows crunching together, starting to fight each other in the middle. 'Taking all that money.'

I nod, I hold onto the door, I have nothing to say. I want to speak to my lawyer.

Harry looks around. The belisha-orange

woodchip wallpaper. The music from the tv room. The rusty mountain bikes in the hall. The pile of unwanted mail and local newspapers. 'So you live here on your own do you?'

'No, with... umm... friends. And my brother. But I wouldn't call him a friend.' And I laugh again like I'm in an interview and I know I'm not going to get the job. They'll ask me about my hobbies in a minute and that'll be the end of it:

Leisure Interests: reading, hang gliding, swimming, body piercing, hill walking, stealing vast sums of money from employers.

Errrr.

'Ah, *family,*' says Harry with a ghost of a smile. A smile that died a few hours previously. 'That must be nice for yehs. Always good to have family.' He is sounding strangely jovial, he must be as nervous as me.

So he knows something.

So he's not used to being in my house.

So I'm freakin him the fuck out.

Basically I can't look him in the eye.

Though it does give me the chance to notice the lovely tiling details in our doorway. It's not the sort of thing you normally bother noticing.

'Come on then, Sunshine. Are yeh not gonna invite me in for a quick cup a tea?'

'Yeah.' I say, wandering back into the house. Towards the kitchen. 'Yeah. No, no, I can't.'

Harry raises his forest of eyebrow question marks.

'Like I said, I'm just about to go out actually.'

'Oh you did. Sorry about that. Anywhere nice?'

'Off into town. Meeting with my brother.'

'Oh he's a nice lad. Met him that one time I did.'

'You did.'

'Yes I did. Seemed very nice enough. So there's not so much chance of us having a wee little chat then?'

Thump thump cardiac arrest.

'What about?'

'Things.'

'Can we not talk tomorrow?'

'Aye we can if yeh in early. But is that likely with you off gallivanting t'night? Just a quick word, that's all I'm asking, Sunshine.'

'What's all this then?' says a familiar voice. A familiar nosey parker edging her snout into whatever trough of gossip she can wedge it into.

'Oh hello there.' Harry's all smiles.

I'm momentarily off my guard. Harry side-steps past me and shakes hands with Sheena like she's a popstar he's always wanted to meet; like he's a customer she wants to impress.

'I don't think we've been introduced,' says Sheena and laughs for no reason I can work out.

I do the honours, 'Sheena, Harry my boss. Harry my boss, Sheena.'

They say things about me I almost don't bother hearing,

'Yeh must have your work cut out getting this one ta do things for yeh.'

I notice Sheena's managed to get herself casually dolled up for this little night out. The hand-me-down-baggy jeans say: I've not really paid any attention to what I'm wearing. The D&G label says: but I have spent ridiculous amounts of money. The size-of-a-seven-year-old orange t-shirt casually invites you to check out her tits. The *fcuk* sentence printed in ever decreasing typeface invites you to stare a while longer. Harry can't resist. Sheena pulls the shirt out to let him have a proper look. He lets out a surprised howl of laughter, pushes his glasses back up his nose.

'It's very good that, very amusin.'

'Makes me laugh. Makes people stare that's tha funny thing. Tryin ta work out what it says.'

'Have yeh seen this, Sunshine? Have yeh seen what it says?' Harry wants me to join in the celebration of tit-tastic scriptwriting.

'No, I've not looked.'

'Any road,' says Sheena. 'It was real nice meetin yeh, Harry. Have to pop roond some time when I'm not goin out. Have ourselves a proper ole chinwag.'

'That'd be grand, right. I'll keep yeh ta that.'

She'll have to watch out. He will come round. And he'll expect a new piece of tit art each time.

Theo's words about me not being jealous zip through my mind like hungry mice trying to escape from a maze. Of course I'm jealous, I'm just not sure of whom and why and of what. I'm just generally jealous of everyone from goldfish to armed robbers. They all seem to know what they're up to: swimming, eating, pointing guns and robbing.

Sheena stands out on the front step protecting her eyes from the sudden burst of low evening sunlight.

'The thing is,' says Harry, leaning forward to whisper. 'If we could just have a quiet word somewhere private.'

'Look, Harry. Y'know, life goes on,' I wish I could

stop smiling and giggling pathetically. 'I've really got to go and get changed. Goin out in a minute, like I said.' I pull my face like a boss explaining why you can't have a pay rise.

'Why don't you ask Harry if he wants to come with us?' Sheena pipes up from outside, mobile clamped to the side of her face but still ready to do us the favour of interrupting.

'Why that'd be a lovely idea, thanking you kindly,' says Harry.

'No no, I don't really think it'd be your sort of place, Harry. It's all loud music and ...' I have no idea, I've never been there; from past experience it'll be expensive foreign lager, boys in sideburns, girls in glitter make-up. Bare flesh everywhere, flirting, fighting, dancefloor fornication. Harry'll probably love it. He'd pay good money to see girls like that half naked. Girls like Sheena.

'Not your scene,' I say. The battle already lost.

'Ah it's a canny little place that BaaBaa,' says Sheena. 'And these haircuts are all the rage now y'know.' She comes over and rubs her hand over Harry's babypink bald head. 'All the footballers havin it shaved off like this.' She gives it another gentle rub. 'Have all the girls after yeh.'

Harry seems to grow an inch in height, 'I can still shake a leg y'know, if the need arises.'

She's twenty-five, he's a hundred-and-sixty - or forty or something - and it has to be said, she isn't interested, but I doubt he's got the dicksense to realise.

'I bet yeh can, aye,' says Sheena, backing away. 'Yeh only as old as the woman yeh feel, isn't that right?' she says breaking into her trademark raucous laugh.

And really, anyone in their right mind would be tempted to lock her in the cellar until she gets all that happiness out of her system. Still happy after four days, Sheena? Any more pathetic woman-you-feel witticisms you'd like to share? No? Come on then. And let that be a lesson to you, young lady.

With a final pathetic joining-in-laugh I quickly buzz off upstairs, half running into Axel as he comes down. Axel smelling of sexually ambiguous toilet water and dressed in a t-shirt as tight as Sheena's and lilac three-quarter length pants that any sane man would be ashamed of wearing in bed. He's also wearing sandals. Which I happen to find vaguely offensive. Though without going into a patent-leather-sandals-as-a-child flashback scene it'd be too complicated to explain why.

'We gonna make tracks, Sib?' he says to me. Him and his *ha ha ha* funny Sib thing. The first time? The second time? The six billionth time? No. Not even the first. Not even a snigger.

'I've just got to get my coat and put my eyeliner on,' I say, going past, thinking, I'll put my old fox fur coat on. As a protest. I usually wear it as a protest against protesters, today I'll wear it as a protest against unnecessary beachwear.

'I make it you got three an a haff and countin,' Axel shouts up at me.

I unlock my bedroom door and try to do some alternate nostril breathing exercises. Breathe in with the left and hold, hold, hold. Now let the air out of the right. Slowly, slowly, slowly. It's not really the right time but apart from a quick bout of self-mutilation I can't really think of anything else that's gonna calm me down and take my mind off that big steaming pile of money over there. Though vast quantities of vomit inducing alcohol might do the job.

I stop and think.

Someone's knocking at my door.

I look at the carpet of notes I've scattered on the floor like a pools winner with a new puppy.

'Who is it?' I will not panic. I will try not to panic. Oh it's no use.

'Only me, Sunshine.' It's Harry. I'd recognise that wheedling smoke-thick old voice anywhere. Actually I really have no idea how old Harry is. He might not be a day over seventy, I'm just not sure. 'Thought I'd just pop up for a look. Don't want ta be imposing on yehs.'

'It's a bit of a mess.' My back against the door ready to fight if I have to. 'I'm just getting changed.'

'Oh you needn't mind me. Just fancied a look at where you rest your head of a night.'

'Why?'

'Being friendly is all.' Being weird is what.

'I'll see you downstairs.'

'No you're alright, I'll wait up here. I'm a little bit shy, y'know, people I don't know.'

I may as well just hang a sign up on the door: Do Not Disturb, Illegal Activity In Progress. 'Won't be a mo,' I say and dive on the money and start scooping it up. Coins and notes. I don't know what I've done with the brown canvas moneybag. Besides my hands are too shaky to do something complicated like siphoning it all back in there.

I pull the black quilt off my bed and stash the money under it. Go back for the stray Bulgarian coins and Monopoly money. 'Just a tick.'

'You've no need to worry about me. I've seen it all before one way or another.'

There. I pull the quilt back and sit on the lump. A lump you don't have to be a princess to notice. I need to get my cuddly toys out of the cellar to garnish the lump; like you do with a dab of mascara and splodge of glitter when you're trying to disguise a big yellowhead as a sparkling beauty spot. Draw attention by distraction. 'Come in.'

Harry squints round the door. 'Ooh,' he says. 'You've done this place out nice.' I nod. Woodchip wallpaper pre-painted magnolia, a few artsy postcards on the wall, a fish tank, a big double bed, a standard bedsit wardrobe/chest of drawers arrangement. 'Very comfy.'

'It's a bit of a mess in here.' Most of my underwear is hanging off the back of the radiator drying quietly and it's not the sort of underwear you would feel particularly proud of.

The brown canvas moneybag is next to the fish tank. With a red plastic bag of coins next to it. 'Just fancied a look at where you lay your head of a night,' says Harry, nodding as he looks round again. 'So those are the fish then?' he says sounding vaguely excited. 'Your girl downstairs, Sheena, was tellin me all about em. And very nice they are.' He makes a laugh sound. I get up and go over to the window and stand there looking out, sighing philosophically. Like the world itself has some contemplative meaning. 'She was telling me how much you like your little fishies. My uncle William, he was a big fish man. Had his own shop there for a while before it all went wrong.'

'Selling fish?'

'Absolutely. Could get yourself a lovely bit of hake or finny haddock from our William's shop you could.' Harry's still staring in at Judas and Satan, doing a bit of synchronised swimming for him.

'Y'know you really should take a look at the view from up here while you're... err... up here.' Especially as there are no moneybags out of the window. None whatsoever. Harry staring at the fish tank like he's fallen into a trance. Or noticed the moneybag. Or he just can't take his eyes off the dancing fish.

'Harry?'

'Oh, yes,' he comes over to the window and has a quick look out at the nettles in the back garden, the tower blocks in the distance, the mould on the window frame, the wind whistling through the bit where the sash window doesn't quite shut properly, doesn't quite open properly. Harry tells me I should probably get the window sorted out. He says it'll probably fall out next time there's a big gust of wind. I tell him I'll speak to the landlord about it and sigh and we look out again: at the passing seagull; the mattress and newspaper bonfire next door are building; the kids in the alley poking each other with sticks.

'We need to talk about today,' Harry says, looking at me with his weepy eyes, his voice dropping down a register. Dropping the comedy, the friendly, the bullshit. 'Something very strange happened t'day.'

I nod. I'm solemn. I'm about to tell all then my mind springs into gear and I'm grabbing my fox fur coat off the top of the wardrobe and I'm out of there,

'Have a chat while we're in the bar, hey?'

If he's noticed the moneybag, Harry knows exactly what's going on. If he doesn't know what's going on, why does he want to talk to me?

I lock up and we plonk down the stairs and out and across the road to Axel's revving jeep. The top's down and we're ready to roll.

'Stop! Stop!' I'm screaming like a hysterical child on a rollercoaster. 'Stopppppppppp!'

Axel slashes his foot down on the brake pedal. We've only actually travelled about fifty metres down the road. 'What's up? What the hell's goin on?'

'I've left my hair dryer on.'

'Whaaat?' Axel's face is a picture and it's not pretty.

'Won't be a mo.' I'm jumping out before Harry can pipe up with any unnecessary information about how I'm lying my socks off. And I'm running back home. My brain can be very slow to process information but I've finally come to the blindingly obvious conclusion. Harry and the gunman are working together.

Five

Harry and the gunman are working together.

My hand shaking, I jerk the ill-fitting new key in the lock till it opens, push open the front door and 3467 the alarm then pootle my way upstairs, grumbling to myself all the while. Then I'm in my room and the fish think it's food time again. 'Sorry kids, got other things to worry about.'

Kurt looks at me, he doesn't have to speak, he knows a black-eyed look can say more than a thousand words. I scrabble under the quilt and bundle all the money up again. Shove it into a Tesco carrier bag that's just hanging around in one or other of the piles of mess; get the brown canvas moneybag and squidge that in. The Bulgarian coins, the Monopoly money. Then I'm out, and puffing and panting, and down into the cellar. My white elephant pile of bricabrac, weirdly shaped plastic items and asphyxiated cuddly toys. I stash the Tesco carrier bag under the lot. Eventually I'll have to pick the stitching out of Paddington Bear and stuff him full of used notes, but right now I haven't got the time.

I check my complexion in the hall mirror and get out of there. I'll have to gather myself and be cooler than an ice pop if I'm going to get through this. I don't even particularly want the money but I am now officially a criminal. There is no going back. If I have to apply for a passport any time soon that'll be what it says under occupation: criminal.

Criminal. Criminal. Criminal.

And that plays on my mind to the extent that I'm probably going to spend much of the evening in the bathroom, washing my hands due to some compulsive-obsessive guilt complex.

I hoof my way back up the road to the jeep; get greeted with predictable looks and words of disdain and non-amusement from Sheena and Axel. Harry keeps himself to himself; sitting in the back of the jeep looking about as relaxed and unworried as a snowman on a beach in Hawaii.

We arrive with a motherfuckin screech of music and brakepads.

'So ya managed to get yeh self invited into that room at the top of the house then?' Sheena says to Harry in what can only be an attempt at making conversation. She's had fifteen minutes to come up with this one, I'm frankly not impressed. 'Managed to see those *famous* fish.'

Here we go. I won't rise to the bait.

'Oh I saw the fish alright. Very nice they are. Gold in colour mainly.'

'Not just any fish them y'know,' Sheena goes on and blather blather on, as Axel does some exaggerated reversing and sideways parking. 'All of em got names.'

'What's wrong with that?' I have to say.

'I'm just sayin,' she says. 'I think it's quite cute. The way yeh treat em. Like they're made of gold not just like *gold*fish you could win at a funfair.'

'You don't understand so why don't you just...'

'I'm only sayin,' she says again.

'It's not how much you pay for something...' blah blah blah obvious conclusion.

'I'm sayin it's nice, that's all I'm sayin. We used

ta have em at home but they never seemed to last more'n a week. Else the cat'd have em, spike em with her claws.'

I don't say anything. Harry and me are trying to climb out of the back of the jeep. It doesn't have anything as sophisticated as doors. Meanwhile I'm roasting like a pig in my fox fur coat and Harry's eyebrows need a good combing after getting blown about in all that wind. He nods but is more concerned about touching pavement. He's not really used to travelling at those sorts of speeds. He doesn't have many friends that drive open-top jeeps.

We start walking. The bar's over the other side of the canal, sitting on the end of a row of railway arches, all carved out and rebuilt with perspex and steel, then coloured in with all the colours of a Smarties packet to make them appealing to the infant-minded.

I'm more a black hole of Calcutta sort of person, it goes without saying.

Sheena won't stop babbling on, 'All I wanted ta say was yeh can tell there's a lot of care and attention gone into lookin after them.'

'Just wait till yeh have the children,' Harry says for no apparent reason. 'Expect yeh'll spoil them as well. Won't know they're born.'

'They won't be born.'

Ha ha says everyone, ha ha. Sometimes my mood is so black people think I must be joking. Harry smiles and looks embarrassed, Axel juggles his keys.

'Ooooh, Sib,' says Sheena, walking next to me and putting her arm around me in a way that I can only describe as: unusual, disturbing and out of character. 'We was ooonly windin you up, so don't go gettin all misery pants on us. Think it's nice ta see yeh have a pal round once in a while that's all I'm sayin.'

We're walking towards the bar, there's a queue of people waiting outside. I stop while we sort this out,

'What d'you mean by that?'

'I think all Sheena tryin ta say is it's kinda cute how you prepared ta give all this love ta ya fish.' Axel like some American peace envoy, always capable of seeing both sides and having no opinions of his own.

'Or else I'm sayin it'd be nice if yeh could give a bit of this love to your friends an people yeh live with instead of being sarky and narky all the time. That's another way of looking at it.'

'I can't argue with that, can I?' I say giving Sheena one of my robot-controlled smiles. I'll say nothing more, because, you see, Sheena, I'm trying to act normal and relaxed. And because, *She*, you can push it and you can push it, but like that Greek bloke who pushes the rock all the way up the mountain, eventually it's gonna come crashing back down and land on your head with a thump. And in this case I'm the rock that's gonna blah de blah de blah thump rock blah your head.

'What's everyone drinkin then?' asks Harry as we glide past the bouncers into our mirror-ball infested paradise. Sheena goes for a Cheeky Chocolate Monkey cocktail, Axel's on juice. 'How about you, Sunshine?'

'Beer.' No imagination that's my problem. Afraid to take risks. Never do anything out of the ordinary. I'm too afraid to even try alcopops, scared I'll love the taste of ethanol and sugar, get addicted and become an alcopopaholic.

Harry wants Guinness, but he'll be fuckin lucky.

Theo sits in the corner pumping a message into his phone, surrounded by a football team's worth of little cocktail glasses. And by the look of him he's had more than is strictly healthy. He recognises me when I sit next to him but for a moment it seems like his mind is somewhere else, somewhere much slower and sadder than this happy drinking hole.

Meanwhile I'm feeling as hot as a Shetland pony in my fur coat. You have to wonder whose idea it was to be so alternative that I just plain do the opposite of everyone else.

'Thank God you're here.' He hugs me like my brother never does. 'I'm havin a crisis.'

'Hey we're here for you, dude.' Axel shares a lazy high-five and asks my brother what he's drinking. Theo tells him he's had about eleven Multiple Orgasms tonight already. Axel shouts over to Sheena and Harry at the bar, tells them to get my little brother a soda. Sheena nods, busy showing Harry her new phone, Harry looking impressed, typing in numbers and talking to someone while Sheena chats up the barman. She laughs and switches round, saying something to the barman as she affectionately rubs her hand over Harry's scalp. Like he's some bizarre but cute breed of bald dog that she just can't resist touching. Leaving me to wonder if she actually does like him after all. And as she can't possibly, I have to admire her. I could never reach that level of false friendliness without chemical intervention.

Theo says, 'I don't know what's happened to me. I'm a mess,' his voice wobbling. 'I don't know what's going on, can't think straight.' He's actually crying, big grown-up man tears.

Sheena comes over, passing out drinks, then goes back to Harry and the barman to collect the rest and chat some more. Axel crunches an ice cube.

'What you do? She find out?'

Theo nods.

'What?'

'Ahh, it's not even worth talkin about.' Theo sniffs, then blows a big wet one into his mushed up hanky.

Sheena brings more drinks, passes me a bottle of Budvar; Harry behind her, getting ignored now there's some gossip in the offing. 'What's all this?'

'You know I've been seeing Ava for about these past two months or so. Off and on. Getting more *on* as time goes by. Like, about three times a week? Still seeing other people - but she didn't know about that, did she? She didn't ask, I didn't tell her.'

'You never mentioned her to *me*,' I say feeling slightly, hmmm, *peeved*.

'She's not the sort of girl I talk about - like, *talk about*. You know, Axel.'

'Tell me about it. She a quality female, you gotta respect her man.'

'*So*?' I have an intense desire to cut through the whining and backslapping to the inevitable, 'What did you do wrong?'

'What d'you think?'

'Was there an airhostess involved? A netball team or a minor celebrity?'

'I couldn't help myself!' he whines like the spoilt child he still is.

'You never can,' I say like the bitter old age

pensioner I'm fast becoming.

'Ay, Sib, don't be givin the boy a hard time.' Axel raising his eyebrows. 'The guy havin a counselling moment here.'

'And whose fault's that?'

'I'm not... I know. Don't think I haven't - I've just had this conversation with her - she dialled me up when I was on the way here. Nearly drove into a bus stop full of people. Seems Felice wanted to – *I don't know* – some bullshit about making a clean fuckin ... said she had to let her know, as she was Ava's *best friend.* She said, I know you're gettin serious with him so I better tell you... *Honesty.* Honesty ruins everything.'

'Who's Felice?' *Felice?* This is all getting a bit too daytime soap opera for my liking. *Felice* pshaw.

Sheena knows the answer, 'Felice is her best friend. Oh Theo, you're such a silly little boy.'

'I know, I know. Don't need anyone to tell me how stupid I am. How wrong I am. How evil I am. I've worked all that out on my own. And you can bet your arse Ava told me all about what a bad man I am. I had nearly twenty minutes of it. Couldn't get a word in edgeways. Sitting there in my car on hands-free. These things happen, that's all I wanted to say. Yeah, I'm sorry but I'm human. I'm a stupid man. Besides it was only once or twice. And it didn't mean anything then. It was before we got serious. As far as I was concerned she was seeing other people... I don't know why Felice had to be so fuckin honest about it. I mean, Ava, y'know? We're talkin about the woman I could have fuckin willingly married, man.'

'Plenty more fish,' says Axel. Which as any fish

keeper will tell you, is nonsense. I wouldn't swap baby Kurt Kobain for a tank full of Butterflyfish. Now Satan and Lorraine, that'd be a different matter, I'd sell those fat buggers to a fishmonger tomorrow. If the price was right.

'Perhaps you should have...' I start but give up. It's got nothing to do with me. Morality wise I shouldn't really be sitting on top of a mountain chucking rocks. Not now I'm a career criminal.

I wonder if I should buy a car. A cheap one.

Then go on holiday.

Buy a dozen Chocolate Catfish and a six-foot tank.

Give to charity. About ten quid.

Buy some clothes, get my hair done. Purple.

Have a tattoo done on my shoulder. Of a sick and devious snake.

I stand up and wander over to the mirrored door that the sign says leads to the toilets. Harry follows me over, weaving his way past the giggly hen-night girls at the bar. You can tell they're on a hen-night because they're absolutely stinking drunk. And because one of them's wearing a wedding dress with a learner sign stapled to her back. As there's no point trying to avoid him, I hold the door for Harry.

'Thanks very much, Sunshine. Whoa, it is busy in here, isn't it?'

I follow the sign and go up the stairs. Push through the door marked Toilet; Harry follows. At the sinks are a trio of slug-faced blonde beauties applying make-up out of a communal bucket marked Ugliness

Concealer. Or else they're wiping their noses, I don't pay a great deal of attention. I wait for a cubicle.

Harry says, 'I'm not sure I'm in the right place here.'

'Don't you worry,' says Blonde Number One. 'Takes some gettin used to. Should've seen *my* face the first time I came up here. There was this guy havin a piss in the sink. I could've screamed! I wouldn't mind but he only had a tiddler!' The three of them laugh. And I'm tempted to laugh myself, if only at Harry's expense.

'It's very modern,' says Harry. 'Unisex that's the thing. First it was the jeans now it's the lavatories. Who knows where it'll stop. We'll all be the same one of these days, we'll all wake up and we'll be the same. Sharing lavatories, I don't know if I like that idea.'

'You shared at home, didn't you? With your sisters? Or did you go in different fields?'

'The place I live now is all fellas. But like I say, it's the modern world.'

'Harry, just out of interest, how old are you exactly?'

'I'm not a day over forty-three, but I feel more like a hundred-and-seventy-three at the moment. Y'know I think I'm more of a twentieth century man than the one we're livin in at the moment. We'll all be livin on the moon that'll be the next thing.' He grins like he's a funny man. He is a funny man but not in the way he thinks he is. 'Sunshine, is it possible we could have a word up here? While we're up here? I was hoping to catch you at some stage this evening.'

'Yeah sure,' I say brightly, as a man with a face the colour of cheap pink bubblegum comes gurning out of a cubicle, still zipping himself up as he walks to the sink. If it was a men-only toilet he'd doubtless be straight out the door, as there's ladies present he thinks it best to make a show of wiping the piss off his hands, if not off his cock. You can't very well have a unisex bidet without attracting police attention.

'About the money,' says Harry. 'The robbery. I told you to get yer self off home I know, but the *po*lice there wanted to have a word with you. I'm sure they'd've been round your place t'night but I told em I couldn't remember your address. I know where you live by the sight of your house, I just couldn't remember where the piece of paper was I'd written your address down on. Oooh, I tell it like it's a riddle. Has no beginning, no ending, makes no sense at all. What I'm tryin ta say - we've a need to get our story straight. I don't mind tellin yeh, when that big fella come in with the gun I was scared. When the *po*lice were asking the questions they ask I was scared. They said to me, what did he look like? I said, I had no idea. They said to me, what clothes was he wearing, of what type? I told them, I don't look at clothes. I said that was more your avenue of interest.'

'Oh God, you didn't? So now I'm the one that's got to -'

'No no, Sunshine, don't get me wrong. I'm not saying you've got to do anything. Only with those *po*lice fellas they're awful at twisting the words you tell em. Forever changing things round and getting you to say what you didn't even know you knew in the first place. I'm not saying we have to be untruthful...'

Another cubicle empties and I make my move. 'Won't be a minute,' I say, putting everything off for a little bit longer.

Then I'm back out and washing my delicate hands with cheap perfumed soap. There's only me out here now and I'm wondering what's happened to Harry. Chances are I took so long he's gone back downstairs long since. I bob down to take a look under a couple of cubicles. Platform heels, next, more girly shoes, next, black loafers pointing in the opposite pissy direction, next, brand spanking white trainers with the laces undone.

I check then check again. Lots of people have new white trainers, lots of people. Some of the trainers even have those trademark four stripes on the side, like the ones you get off the market. Why would anyone want to follow me? No real reason, other than to stab me and rob me and throw me in a ditch. Perhaps I should be worried. The toilet flushes and the person in the cubicle stands up. Now I really am worried.

Six

Now I really am worried. Really, really bloody fuckin swearword worried. Whoever it is in there, they're gonna come waltzing out any minute. Ready to wash their hands, wring my neck, then wash their hands again. I don't want to be standing round here, waiting to find out who it is. I don't want to be relieved that it's no one I've ever met before. A blind man with bad dress sense. I don't care. I just don't want to know.

Then suddenly a man in a yellow waistcoat, novelty Mickey Mouse dickie-bow and foppish hairstyle comes bursting through from the door and looks at me funny. Like I smell. Like the stench in this toilet is all my fault. I get up off my hands and knees and smile. Neglect to run my hands under the tap and bound off back downstairs to my brother. I hug him again; it seems like the right thing to do in the circumstances. Though he seems slightly put out and disturbed by my touching him, he also appears to have cheered up a bit. So his love affair problems can't be all that bad.

Harry isn't with brother, Axel or Sheena, so it looks like he might be upstairs still, but then I notice him standing at the door like a dog waiting for his master to come home. His wet nose stuck in a bottle of beer. I'm watching the door to the toilet to see who's going to come out but not even my old friend Mickey Bow-tie has come out yet.

'Why don't we leave?' I say to Axel, smiling so he might remember to like me, and forget that I haven't paid my rent this month. 'Must be somewhere more exciting than this we could go to?'

'Yeah, could. There aint no rush.'

Sheena's phone starts bleeping the theme from Jaws; strangely it's for Harry.

Theo says, 'Hey listen, normally with me. Look, sorry to go on about this.'

'No you're cool dude.'

'I need to tell you what I'm thinkin, y'know?'

'Yeah.'

'It goes like - find a girl and she's lovely and you're with it but then you spot another girl that's a different flavour. Like you get off with a blonde that's small and cute and bubbly, then you see this older woman in a business suit, short dark hair, serious face. And that's what you want. Totally absolutely. Like that's what you've *always* wanted. But boredom after twenty four hours is what I'm saying – twenty four days if you're lucky.'

'Uh huh. The way of the world, man.'

'But I guess even if you live in a sweet shop, eventually as you're going through all the sweets you find one that's *so* your favourite, you don't care about nothing else. You don't wanna look for nothing else. It's like this is your favourite favourite sweet and you just want to keep chewing it forever. That's kinda the way I feel about her. About Ava.'

I tell him, 'You want to know the way I see it? This is my analysis...'

I turn round and remember that I was meant to be watching the door that leads up to the toilet. Anyone could have gone in, anyone could have come out. Not that I'm worried. Not that I'm about to get robbed, knifed and thrown in a ditch any time in the next two or three hours. Not while I'm surrounded by all these happy drunken people.

Theo nods his head at me and sniffs like a sad puppy with asthma. 'So what's the great conclusion that you've come to?'

I tell him, 'Brother, you're delusional and lovesick, but that's inevitable. You're a drama queen.' I'm hyper and terrified for no real reason. Lots of people wear cheap white trainers. What am I thinking. So now I've got a list of things I'm pant-wettingly scared off:

> doors opening and closing
> white training shoes
> guns
> death
> clowns
> processed peas
> really big spiders

'Come on, give the guy a break. He tryin ta speak his feelings, get all Oprah with us. This aint what he do normally ya know? Theo don't normally do feelings. Normally he a guy. This kinda stuff, it kinda alien, y'know? We gotta listen when he say it.'

'Sorry, but I *am* listening, and I think it's interesting. The story basically, my little brother is telling is, he's weirdly successful with women, and as a result he's had the opportunity to try every *type* of female there is. On the planet. Correct me if I'm wrong?'

'Not quite what I was -' Grinning his smug little face off.

'But more or less? Tall and short, butch and

femme, blonde and black, sweet and sour, sub and dom, frigid and nympho. And basically, after a couple of hours, days, weeks - you get bored with them?'

'Well... I wouldn't say -'

'That's what he sayin - the way I hear it.'

'All women bore you.'

'I love women, but -'

'You're gay.'

'Get lost.'

'Simple and plain, Theo, you're a pufter. It's taken you two-hundred women to find out but frankly now it's time to move on. You got two options as I see it. Abstinence or buggery. Enter a monastry or enter the life of Sodom.'

'You're so full of it.'

Axel's laughing if Theo isn't, nodding his head like a man who knows a truth that dare not speak its name.

'So let's see if we can't find a nice little chap in here to satisfy your virginal desires.' I head off. Harry and Sheena at the door talking again. My foppish friend in the yellow waistcoat over with some more waistcoated and suited-up chums in the far corner.

Axel reaches across to grab my arm, giving me a serious stare with his smokey eyes, 'Hey Sib, I hope you is jokin here, right?' There's a whisper of a smile on his lips. It's all the encouragement I need.

I make my way through the crowd towards my foppish friend in the Mickey Mouse bow-tie, nudging past people being careful not to spill anyone's drinks as I go fur-coating past. I look back to check brother and friend are watching then stand in front of Mickey and try and catch his eye. I'm wondering if I can just stand here and nod my head: make it look like I'm talking to Mickey. I don't actually want to talk to him. That's probably the last thing I want to do. I'd rather have furry spiders crawl over my body. I mean *strangers,* unattractive strangers especially, why would anyone want to talk to them? Besides, he's not paying me a blind bit of notice, too busy pontificating to one of his suited-up accomplices about the state of the nation. It's in a bad way apparently.

I'm standing so close to him that he'll have to notice me but it must be pretty obvious to Axel and Theo that I'm being ignored, that Mickey's not looking at me or even thinking about talking to me.

So I have two choices. I can fail to say anything and go back and admit to my brother what a scaredy cat I am. Or I can actually speak to Mickey and find out if he thinks my brother is shaggable or not...

There has to be some other way...

The thing is... I'm conducting a test. An experiment in behaviour. Behavioural psychology, actually. Would you mind me asking you a few questions about whether or not you fancy my brother or not. I mean you are gay, aren't you? Or bisexual at least, I mean, it's pretty obvious.

Mickey stops and looks at me. Like I'm speaking aloud the thoughts in my head. He looks at me in such a way that it appears he is expecting me to say something,

'Hello again,' I say. 'How are you?' Which is the most pathetic thing I could come up with in the circumstances.

Is it any wonder I don't have any friends? Is it any wonder I get on better with fish than people when this is the best I can do?

Mickey looks at me like I'm a freak, a genetic mutation. Which from him I take as a compliment, '*Sorry?*'

I smile and nod. So this is what it feels like to be a rabbit stuck in the middle of the road with angry headlights approaching from all directions. 'I wondered if I could just ask you a question,' I say, I shrug, I giggle and squirm like the village idiot I am.

He cocks his head towards me, waiting. He's confused by my mild manner. I look like a banshee but I sound like a lost child in a supermarket, ready to burst into tears at any moment if someone doesn't help and rescue me. But there's no real need for me to be lacking in confidence. At the very worst he can shout at me, hit me, throw a drink at me, or humiliate me and turn me into a laughing stock. But that's just an average day at work for me. I just need to convince myself that I don't really have to care. That he doesn't matter. So I can talk to him with confidence, not the catatonic tongue-binding fear I feel whenever I try and talk to someone I fancy.

He's still waiting for the question.

'Do you know where the toilets are?'

'*What?*' Stupid. That's not a sensible question. He looks at me like he thinks I might be followed by hidden cameras. This red-haired monstrosity in a fur coat and a sheen of unnecessary sweat.

'I mean... do you know –' I have to shout so he can hear me above the plonk-plonk disco music and the screaming hen party '- where the library is?'

'Sorry?'

'The library? I'm meeting someone... near there.'

So there we go, speaking to people is easy after all. Speaking sense is harder, but if you just open your mouth, words will come.

'Why the *fuck* are you fucking asking me?'

Why am I asking him? He's suprisingly hard-faced and potty-mouthed is Mickey. I'm a bit at a loss to be honest.

'You look like someone who reads books,' I say, smiling my silly head off.

If I was on drugs you could understand it. If I was educationally subnormal it'd be acceptable. From a red-haired, fox-furred, sweat-covered loon, the man is clearly entitled to be ever so slightly *unnerved.*

'What on earth are you talking about?' If his brow was any more knitted he'd be wearing a jumper on his face.

'Is it over there?' I turn round and point in the general direction of my brother and friends. Theo and Axel standing with their jaws hanging open. Sheena walking back over to them but looking over like she's asking what's going on. 'Is it in that sort of direction?'

I should work in Public Relations. I could do what Sheena does, I could schmooze and press flesh, I could try it for a day and cry my way home on the train.

'As far as I'm aware,' says Mickey, 'it's actually in that direction.' He points towards the toilets but I'm pretty sure the library isn't in there.

'Oh great. Thanks for all your help, that's been great. Thanks.'

'No problem, any time.'

His friends carry on staring at me like they've got nothing better to do. I smile and repeat the smile more when I see Sheena standing next to Theo laughing her head off. In fact her head is laughing so much it might just fall off any second.

I notice Harry is no longer standing at the door and he's not with brother and friends. This lightens my mood enormously and cheers me up so much I go to the bar to get another round of drinks in.

I go back over to my so-called *gang* with my carefully balanced round of drinks - paid for with my ill-gotten booty. Making them as guilty as me. In a karmic sense. Though I doubt the police would be very interested.

Theo and Axel call me all sorts of names and swear at me but want to know exactly what Mickey the Fop thought of them. Thankfully I find it easy to lie outrageously, 'He liked you, Axel. He said you had lovely bone structure. But he didn't fancy you, lickle brother. He said you were too dull looking.'

'What d'you mean *too dull looking*?'

'Don't ask me, go and ask *him.*'

'Dull looking? What does *dull looking* mean? Not clever enough or *dull* looking?'

'Sib only windin you up is all.'

'He didn't say that did he?'

Sheena cackles like a goose that's laid a nuclear egg. 'Give over. Didn't say nothing of the sort. Probably asked about, I dun know, what football team he supports, the weather or summat.'

'He fancied you,' I tell her, allowing her to smile. 'And he agreed that Axel was very attractive from a distance. Like a Monet, beautiful from across the other side of the room, just a bit of a splodgy mess when

74

you get too close up.'

'Give over you. I'll go an ask him then,' she says it like it's a challenge. But no one really cares if Sheena talks to strange men. With me it's an established fact that I'm sulky and withdrawn. And now it's a newly established fact that my brother's gay, but he's not used to being rejected, even by floppy fringed numptys in vomit-yellow waistcoats. The man Sheena has now decided to go and talk to. Who seems much happier talking to her than he was when I asked him to give me directions to the library. Turn left at the toilets, yes thank you, Mickey. So I carry on giving Theo a hard time. It's a habit, it passes the time, it makes a change from worrying about getting stabbed to death and thrown in the canal.

'He didn't like you, brother. This is gonna be a whole new set of challenges for you. You're gonna have to smarten yourself up a bit if you wanna be a boy toy.'

'You think you're so clever.'

'You're the genius of the family.'

'And you're the big head know-it-all.'

'Hey hey, kids. Let's be *cool*.' Axel flashes his ice white smile at us both. But really we're just like puppies learning how to fight. We enjoy it, we don't mean it. At least I don't.

Theo's on the offensive, 'Think you're so bloody superior. Listen, if you're so good at talking to people you can do me a favour and speak to Ava for me. God knows she won't talk to me.'

So it goes back to him and his troubles. Is now the time to bring up the gun at the head incident, the masked man in his white trainers following me everywhere? My boss who thinks I've got a bag of stolen money hidden away in my sock drawer.

'You gotta help me get her back,' he goes on, this time he's hugging Axel. Axel looks at me like - what can you do? - the thing is little brother's had too many Multiple Orgasms tonight, that's the problem. He can't think straight – as I pointed out earlier. So I decide to be generous, help him out.

'Tell me what I can do and I'll do it.' What do *I* care. About this Ava that is. Of course I care about my little chedder cheese moon of a brother. I remember the first time I clapped eyes on him, he was crying and full of shit even all those years ago. He wipes away a little tear.

'I haven't got a clue what anyone can do.'

'We need a plan,' I tell him. 'Have you got a picture of her or anything?'

Theo nods, 'Here. In my wallet.' He really is in a state. He stops to blow his nose, then hands me a picture. I quickly wipe the goss off with my sleeve and take a look. I have seen her, as it happens, I think I just happened to be hanging around outside and she went past. I was emptying the bin or counting the dandelions in the front lawn. I was busy anyway. She went floating past. That was a few weeks ago. Never seen her since. Didn't think she was anyone special. Slim, dark, attractive in the way a shiny plum is attractive but a battered prune is interesting. You'd look at her once and be impressed but there'd be nothing to look back for. Though she does have an incredible nose, slightly bent, slightly larger than she needs for basic breathing purposes. The sort of nose that a young woman like her probably hates, but that sits there like a large stone in a Zen garden: it draws your attention, but shows off how simple and beautifully arranged everything else is around it. Though she'll no doubt go and spoil it as soon as she can afford to and have a tiny little button nose fitted, but that's the modern world for you, as my Mum would probably say in a completely different context.

'She's beautiful, isn't she?' says Theo in his choked Multiple Orgasm drained voice. We have no option but to agree.

Axel says, 'Hey, y'know bud, we really should be gettin you home.'

Theo waves him away, 'I'm driving, I can go home on my own. I can give you a lift,' he says to me. 'It's not a problem. Look at her. Look at her and tell me she's not beautiful.'

'She's not beautiful.'

'I hate you.' He doesn't know whether to hit me, cry or fall over.

'Joking.' I smile and give him another of these strange uncomfortable hugs he seems to like so much. Looking at her for the last time I have to say that despite all her bland almost-perfection, she does have something. Aside from a face that resembles a garden made of stones and raked sand.

She's got eyes like a Disney princess.

You can do a lot with eyes. Cleopatra was probably a real hummer but she had eyes that could turn a grown man to gelatine and a grown horse to glue.

'Hey,' says a familiar foghorn voice. 'Look who I found again.' Sheena dragging Harry over. 'Got someone else wants to see you an all.'

Not the man in the yellow waistcoat. Please God

not the man in the yellow waistcoat.

And if seconds could be broken down into freeze-frame finishing-line camera time there's a brief lip-curling-into-a-smile moment where I'm pleased that it isn't Mickey the Fop with his sleeves rolled up ready to biff me one. Then time hurtles on and I realise my mistake.

Charlie Strange has decided to come for a drink with us.

Seven

Charlie Strange has decided to come for a drink with us. Now more than ever before in my life, I want to be alone with my brother.

'We better get you home then, Theo. Had a bit too much to drink I reckon,' and I do that false laughing thing I've started doing recently. Ha ha ha ha ha. Desperation and buckling of knees. Nobody moves; everybody smiles.

'Hi, I'm Axel,' says Axel. 'How ya doin, man.' He holds out his hand to shake, Charlie Strange nods but says nothing.

'Ha ha ha,' it seems I'm laughing again. I've got nothing to say.

'Whose round is it then?' asks Sheena. 'When we've all got a drink I'll tell yeh what those fellas over there have just been sayin ta me.'

'Sheena,' my little brother says with a quiver in his little voice, 'do you think I'm a bastard? You're a woman. Me and you - when we - did I treat you like a piece of meat? Like a sweet shop. Like a - am I an idiot? Tell me. Don't tell me I'm drunk I know I'm bloody fuckin drunk. What am I doing wrong? Why does she hate me? I fuckin love her. Why does she hate me, Sheena?'

'Because you slept with her best friend.'

'Yeah but apart from that.'

'There is no apart from that.'

'We'd better get you home,' Axel takes a lead, picks up Theo's phone, his car keys, his wallet; takes him by the arm. 'Here,' he says to me, 'You're drivin.'

'What?'

'This guy in no state t'drive.'

'He can pick it up in the morning, can't he? When he's sober-er.' There's worry, fear and panic in my voice.

'Leave *his* car round here till tomorra mornin? Won't be no car. Be space. Be dust. You drivin it, come on.'

'What about...' panic panic. This is an excuse for me to leave, why am I panicking? 'I only passed my test... seven years ago.'

'You be fine.'

'I haven't driven for... seven years.' I'm clutching at straws. 'I've been drinking.'

'You only had a bottle an a haff. Look,' he whispers to me, lets go of Theo. Theo hugs Harry and tells him his troubles. Harry looks as uncomfortable at being touched as only a forty-three year-old confirmed bachelor can. Then Theo tries to hug Charlie Strange. Charlie looks at him with those eyes, and Theo gets the message. He's drunk, but he's not mental. Axel says, 'Think Sheena found a couple a new friends.' He nods over at Mickey the Fop and the suits in the corner. 'You can't be makin her leave, Sib. Girl gotta have her fun, y'know. She work hard, she need to let go every now an again. An I know what you gonna say, but listen, Sheena aint been happy recently. All relationship traumas an shit. You hear all that about her an that guy at work? Some boss guy she goin with, an he married an all the usual bullshit.'

I shake my head, of course not, I didn't hear a thing.

'Here,' he presses Theo's car keys into my hand, folds my fingers over them. Firmly. Looks me in the eye. 'Do it. I see you back there. 'Kay? He just parked out front, ya can't miss it.'

'Oh, Sunshine,' says Harry as I watch Axel drag Theo off into the distance, watch Sheena say her goodbyes and make her happy-happy way back over to her circle of suited-up and novelty bow-tied admirers. 'If you're goin back that way is there any chance you could give us a lift back to The Naughty Squirrel? Only we're not really great big fans of this establishment, if you understand. Prefer to be back on turf we're more well accustomed to. Of course you're very welcome to join us for a drink or two in there. I'm not saying we're trying to get rid of you. Quite the opposite.'

Charlie Strange smiles, he smiles like an executioner about to pull the lever.

'Harry, I'd really *love* to give you both a lift, but there isn't room. It's not really a car with space for passengers.'

'*What?* Has it only the one seat? Is it a racing car?' Harry puts on his I'm-a-funny-man face.

'And also... I'm not actually going directly home or in that direction at all.'

'Where is it yer goin?' asks Charlie. 'I wouldn't mind goin for a drive me self. Don't mind much where we go. I like a change. Go to Blackpool as far as I'm concerned.'

'Thought I might pop in on my Mum and Dad,' I say. I say the first thing that comes into my mind.

'And where do they live?' asks Charlie.

'The Lake District,' I say, trying to be realistic. The first thing that came into my head - I was going to say - the Andes. I wanted Charlie to say, 'Where are the Andies?' And then I'd say, 'On the end of the Wristies!' And that'd be hilarious, up until and almost including the bit where he grabs my red hair and shakes me till my teeth fall out.

'The Lake District?' says Harry. 'Is that not a bit of a long way, what with you having to be in work tomorrow?'

'Well, I wasn't planning on staying long. Just fancied a chat.'

'Sure, you can talk to us,' my boss tells me, patting me on the back and keeping his hand there, guiding me towards the door. 'If yeh wants ta talk to ya Mammy and Daddy yeh can always give them a ring on the old dog an bone. I'm sure they'd love to hear from you. No matter what time of day or night.' Harry walks by my side, Charlie following behind us. It seems he isn't in the mood for chatting.

Theo's car, a red sports roadster, Japanese, but I'm not quite sure what sport you're meant to play in it. There isn't much room in the back for a tennis racket, let alone a cricket team. Two bucket seats and a shelf, that's what I was trying to explain to Harry. And it accelerates with the force of a car crash. If you're not buckled into the seats you'll flop about like an anaesthetised tongue. Or at least that was the way I felt when Theo took me for a *spin* and I forgot to put my safety braces on. Next time I was strapped in tight, stuck to my chair like a suckerfish.

It's parked over the other side of the road and Axel's right, people are paying it too much attention, looking at it as they go past. Couples, guys in groups, stopping, having a quick look inside. Good upholstery, wall-to-wall carpets, what a lovely gear-stick. I wouldn't mind getting my hands round that. It's a car that even Theo isn't rich enough to afford, but the bank were stupid enough to give him a loan and he bought it second-hand at an auction in Belgium. He reckons it's a total babe-magnet, but I think most women would prefer a nice new pair of shoes. It's the blokes that start dribbling over it like it's a pouting wet vulva. A car like this isn't a penis-extension; it's a vagina-on-wheels. Anyone with a cock can't help but want to be inside it. Passing lesbians have probably been rubbing themselves against it all evening. It even excites me, though it scares me a million times more. Needless to say, I've ridden in it three times, twice in the passenger seat, once folded up like a flat-pack self-assembly cupboard on the shelf in the back.

'Is that it?' Harry can hardly believe his luck. 'Ho ho. What d'yeh think of that then?' he asks Charlie Strange.

'Is it yours, is it?'

'No, it's the brother's. Is it not a fine piece of machinery?'

'I'll not argue with you there.'

People tend to think they have to go heavy with the compliments before they try and get inside. It's the least they can do, you can't treat a car like this like some common taxi you pick up in the street: get in, have a quick ride, pay your money, never see it again in your life.

Prostitutes, taxis. Taxis, prostitutes.

I can't be the first person to notice.

The point being, if mini-cabs are hookers, then this car is a gorgeous girl from a respectable family who goes like the clappers if you treat her right. And as I travel almost everywhere by bus that means that I like to engage in massive if slightly dull orgies and my favourite colour is red. Which makes some kind of sense. In a parallel universe far *far* away. Though it's probably best if I delete that thought and never mention it again.

Then, as if to back it all up, Theo has given his car a woman's name. He said to me, 'I've decided to call her Octavia.'

'Octavia? *Her?* Well that makes sense.'

'I wouldn't expect you to understand.'

'Well I don't.'

'Well I wouldn't expect you to.'

'Good.'

'Good.'

I beep the alarm button on the end of the key fob.

Octavia winks her lights at me cheekily.

If I just get in there and start licking the seats, will anyone mind?

'Ho ho.' Harry like he's never seen or been in a car for the past ten or twenty years.

'Grand,' says Charlie Strange.

I gently wrench open the driver's door and throw my coat in, my *pals* go round the other side. Charlie gets in the back, squeezing himself in on top of my fur coat, Harry sitting to the right of me, because, one reason why this car was cheap enough for a cheapskate like my brother to afford. The driver sits in the same place they would if they were driving it in Tokyo. Which is: the left-hand side, not Yokomura Road, two blocks down from Tokyo High Street.

Right nostril, breathe in.

84

And hold. Hold. Hold.

And ... ahhhhh.

Left nostril in, hold hold hold.

'Is everything alright?' asks Harry sounding concerned.

'Oh. Yeah. What? Excellent.' And of course, I laugh.

I check the rear-view mirror. Charlie Strange's hot green eyes. Mirror, indicate, panic, manoeuvre. And I decide to fuck it all and show Octavia who's boss. It's how she likes it; it's what she's used to. Being abused in a loving way. High-class whore that she is. 'Buckle up and hold tight.' I flick the cd player on, packed with conversation-destroying Motorhead. 'Don't make records like this any more,' I say, cranking it up to piss off my passengers to maximum effect. Gingerly edging my way out onto the road. Then buoyed by my marginally over-the-limit one-point-five bottles of Budvar I put my foot to the floor. Our heads flip back like table footballers, and I'm tempted to scream with fear and exhilaration, instead I shout along with Lemmy.

About how we know we're going to lose. About gambling being for idiots. But y'know, what the heck, that's the way we like it, isn't it? We don't want to exist on this astral plane for ever. And something about a joker. Diddle diddle dee, diddle diddle dee, diddle diddle dee. Duh duh duh. Duh duh duh. Duh. Huh. *Duh.*

Luckily being bald Harry has no qualms about going grey. Outside The Angry Squirrel and he's had enough of being trapped inside my brother's red-hot vagina-mobile. It was the overtaking that did it. I wanted to go fast, I wanted to overtake, but I'm on the pavement side, he's the only one that can see if anything's coming. 'Is anything coming?' vroom vroom.

'No, I mean, hang on, yes, oh God, no*ooo*!'

When you're bludgeoning through the speed limit like I was, you need instant answers. Harry's more of a measured horse and cart kind of navigator. Not enough space invaders and go-kart racing in his youth. I didn't have enough either but it seems I'm suddenly making up for it. Playing Russian Roulette in a borrowed car.

'Are yeh alright in there? Your legs gone asleep?' Harry asks Charlie Strange.

'No no, I'll be right for a while longer.'

'Y'not getting out here then? Not fancy a quick Shandy Bass?'

'No, I'm figuring it'll be alright for me to get myself a lift a wee bit further on. I'm not really in the mood for more drinkin.'

'Yeh surprise me,' says Harry, raising his eyebrows. 'Is that alright with you is it, Sunshine?'

'Errr...' Is it possible for me to say, fuckin no fuckin way. And still appear to be the calm, rational and innocent person I clearly am not.

'It's not so far,' says Harry, pushing the door to. 'See yeh bright and early tomorra mornin then. Remember what I said about those *po*lice fellas.' He slams the door.

Charlie is breathing down my neck.

Why did I decide to fall in love with the most dangerous man in the city? And then steal all his ill-gotten gains. He says, 'I hear you had a bit of trouble t'day at work.'

'Yes.'

'That must have been a bit... unnerving.'

'Yes.'

He nods, I watch in the mirror. His eyes like a cat that's been guzzling amphetamine-laced milk. Still with his gold rope chain round his neck, his scabby scar on his cheek, his beautiful fudge-coloured skin and no shirt, his pinstriped jumble-sale accountant's suit, his missing teeth, his brand spanking but slightly scuffed white trainers; wedged like a ready-to-drop embryo on the back shelf of my brother's vaginamobile.

'Where to?' I ask like the prostitute-taxi driver I am.

'Down the road a ways.' He points vaguely.

'You'll have to give me directions,' I say, my voice bright like broken glass.

Charlie Strange says nothing. Then I'm driving, driving too far, too straight, too fuckin-clearly-nowhere near where he lives.

I say, 'I didn't know you lived in this part of town?'

'I don't.'

'Oh.'

I'm still driving, going through traffic lights, stopping at roundabouts, asking, 'Is it straight across here?' Charlie Strange nods whatever I say.

'I think we better turn back,' I say. He doesn't nod. I slow down and lean across, trying to see if there's anything coming, before I try and do my film star u-turn. Charlie puts his hand on my shoulder.

'Stop the car,' he says.

I stop the car. He tells me to open the door and get out. I do as I'm told. We're not in countryside but we're in big house suburbia. Front doors at more than shouting distance. Charlie tells me to push the seat forward, then he's climbing out and stretching his legs.

'Think I must have been dreamin,' he says. 'Enjoyed the journey s'much. Would it not be possible for me to have a little drive me self? Would that not be possible?'

I shake my head.

'At least sit behind the wheel and get a feel for it?' he says.

I nod.

'Take it for a quick spin, how about that?'

I don't nod.

'That's grand of you. Lovely pretty thing it is.'

He slams the door shut and revs the engine. He smiles and waves, screeches into gear and puts his foot down. Goes. Gets to the end of the street and reverses. He comes back. Fast. Making Octavia squeal he's so rough with her. He stops, buzzes the window down. 'I think you owe me a favour.' He looks at me with those green eyes that would have Egyptians worshipping him. 'I won't be long,' and this time he goes and this time when he gets to the end of the road he indicates left and goes right. He doesn't come back, at least not right away. But of course I'm prepared to wait. I've just allowed someone I sort-of-know to steal my brother's red sports love-mobile. He's fuckin her brains out while I stand here in the increasingly cold suburban air, thinking, he's only joking. Thinking, I should have asked him for my coat, he won't want that.

Thinking, he's only doing it to wind me up. He'll be back in a minute. I'll just give him another fifteen minutes, then I'll call a taxi. Or perhaps then, I'll have to walk for miles, find a phonebox, and try and describe roughly where I am.

'I'm near some houses and they're very big. It's on the 273 bus route. It's a nice area.'

The minute I start walking he'll come back. So on that reckoning I should start walking straightaway. Or else there's no point in moving. I'm not sure. But as it starts to get colder and colder and I start to feel more and more stupid, it does seem like there is no point in me just standing here. Like a lemon.

So I start walking.

So I carry on walking.

Then I keep on carrying on walking. I keep looking back though. Like I just have to make sure. Maybe if he loves me enough he'll come back and rescue me. So I carry on keeping on walking, even though I'm sure he will come back eventually. Of course he will. He's probably only playing a joke, having a bit of a laugh. Of course he'll come back. The only question is when.

Eight

If the only question is when. The only answer is never. Three miles, four miles, how far have I walked in the past hour and five minutes. And by now the odds on Charlie Strange coming back are slightly less than the odds on Jesus making a return visit. I know who I'd put my money on... and at least he'd have some fish, bread and a nice bottle of wine in his pocket.

Luckily as I made absolutely no turns right left or for the better, it's easy for me to navigate my way towards a busier part of town, towards a phonebox where I can order an expensive taxi to come and take me home. Where I can sob all night and think of ways to solve what is going to be an especially difficult 7:00am *countdown conundrum*. Brother gets up for work, wonders where his car is... and I tell him... what exactly?

Luckily by then I'll have been down the Early-Morning Car-O-Mart and traded my bag full of money for an almost identical red sports roadster. Theo won't notice that the registration number's changed or that the steering wheel's moved or that this is the cheaper version vaginamobile as made by Ford with an extra two doors for added comfort and accessibility. And that it's blue like a cold finger not red like a poker that's been resting too long in the fire. Errrrr. Etc etc etc. Errrrr.

Whoever said: There is always a solution to any problem. Whoever said: Don't look on difficult situations as problems consider them to be opportunities. Whoever said that: deserves a good slapping.

90

I phone Ab's Cabs, speak to the Taxi Madam; I've got a vague idea where I am. I tell her I'll be standing on the edge of the road waving. 'Red hair,' I say. I tell her to hurry cos I'm freezing. I tell her some friends dropped me off. I tell her it's a practical joke and that's why I don't know where I am. 'At all!' I say. Ha ha ha. 'Haven't got a clue!' Ho ho ho. She talks to someone in the background but she doesn't find it very funny. I'm laughing of course; I'm a walking hyena these days. The Taxi Madam suggests I dial the operator and explain the situation, see if they can match the phone number to the location, then give her a call back.

So next thing I know. Next thing, forty-five minutes later, I'm sitting in the back of a mini-cab winging my way back to South Central. And I am definitely going to spend every penny of that bloody money now. It's mine. I deserve it. The car thing is simple. I say, I drove it back. It must have been stolen when it was parked outside. I'll say, yes, I put the krook-lock on, yes, I activated the demobiliser, set the alarm. They're very sophisticated these days, car thieves, I'll say. They're like ghosts; they can get in whatever you do. They steal to order these days, I'll say. I'll say that because that's what they always say on the television news. If only I could convince myself, I might stand a chance of fooling my little brother.

And to think how happy I was when I was poor. Life was so much easier then. Perhaps I should take the money into work tomorrow. When Charlie Strange comes in, say, oh, *Charlie Strange*, you left this here yesterday. Don't know what's in it, think it might be a corned beef sandwich. If you don't want it, I'll have it.

I get home and 3467 the alarm.

We're a household in an almost constant state of alarm. So long as you don't open the front door, the back door, go in the tv room, or the kitchen, you're okay. You can never be too careful is our attitude. If you're not careful – like I never am - if you trip over the bikes as you make your way to deactivate the bleeping sonic timebomb - that's when you have a problem. All hell breaks loose. Axel appears at the top of the stairs with a baseball bat. The neighbours bang on the wall. Which is nice of them. In effect they're saying – hey, if you're gonna burglarise someone try and and do it a bit more quietly, we're trying to sleep/ mow the lawn/watch tv here. Then I apologise to everyone, Sheena tells me she nearly had a heart attack, baby brother gets woken up by all the shouting blah de blah de blah de la la.

Luckily this time I get there in time, I get the numbers right and the world sleeps on as if I didn't exist.

I trudge my way up the stairs. Axel's light's still on, but he's probably afraid of the dark. I go up the next flight to my room, put the key in the lock and try and turn it. It isn't locked. I push open the door and switch on the light, stand in the doorway, look at the fish yawning, slowly getting out of bed to come and gape at me. Complaining about getting woken up so early.

I'm almost certain, I'm almost seventy-five

percent certain, I'm pretty sure I remembered to lock my door. I have no idea if I remembered to lock my door. If I knew, I could be certain, if I was certain, I could know. 'Hello,' I say quietly like I don't want anyone to hear. There aren't so many hiding places in my room. The big bundled up pile of duvet falling off the bed – a small child could be hiding in there, or a family of beavers.

The wardrobe or behind the door.

I push the door till it's flat against the wall. Unless I am dealing with a supernatural force there is no one behind the door. However once you start getting paranoid anything seems possible. I go over to the wardrobe and knock, and then knock again. 'Is there anyone in?' There's a big pile of laundry in the bottom that'll fall out when I open the door.

I turn the lock, open the door. The laundry falls out. And to think that previously I had dreams about Charlie Strange falling out of my closet.

The problem is it's too untidy in here for me to notice if someone else has been in here making a mess. It smells of cigarettes, though that might just be Harry. If anything it looks a bit tidier in here than before. Though if some tidy person has been in here snooping around they could have picked up those socks and taken those cups down.

I'm not in a sleeping mood, I'm worried about small children and wild animals hiding in my duvet, ghost thieves hiding behind the door. I decide to go downstairs and make some toast, have some cheese to make me dream. Then I decide that the first and most sensible thing to do would be to go down into the cellar and look at my money for a while. It's become a thing I like to do, flick through the tens, look at the picture on the back of the fifties, pocket a couple of twenties. Then I decide it's time I did something about this bag of money so I go back to my original plan and get the penknife and cut open the stitching between Paddington Bear's legs and pull out the stuffing from his torso, pack him with fivers and seal him back up with holly-and-ivy Christmas sellotape. Put him back, as innocent as a cuddly toy, with the rest of his friends in the asphyxiating plastic bag. Then I shove as many of the coin bags as I can into the enormous pot piggy bank and leave the remainder in the Tesco carrier bag. Now I can feel happy enough to make my cheese on toast.

On my way back up I stop outside Axel's room. I'm going to have to tell someone about something. I need to talk and Sheena's probably off performing gymnastics with some floppy-fringed fop. Then there's Baby Kurt, he'd give me the usual yes or no answers I don't want to hear. I knock then knock again.

'Hey? Yeah?' sleepy voice.

'It's me.'

''Kay. One minute.' Axel drags himself out of bed and answers the door. Boxer shorts and socks. He wears socks in bed, wears sandals on the street. 'What's up?'

'Can I have a word?'

He scratches a hairless armpit, turns his back for me to follow, 'One word? How about *vomit*?'

'Huh?' I'm still in the doorway looking in at red painted walls, red spot lighting, African wall masks, fat statues of Buddha and assorted third world haberdashery and bricabrac.

Axel stops, turns back to explain, 'Your cute little brother? Here's me goin on about you and drinkin? Turns out I lookin at the wrong member of family. Hey, you better come in. We don't wanna be wakin up *sleepin beauty* next door. Though I reckon it'd take world war fuckin *seven* to get his ass outta bed.' He goes over to the mini-disc player and puts on some ethnic sheep-counting music. I stand on the woven rug in the middle of the room. Axel grabs a big cushion and parks his butt on the floor, grabs another off the bed and puts it next to him like an invitation for me to go and sit by his side; slouching, cross-legged like a tired yogi, messing in his drugs box, 'I wipe vomit off the jeep. I wipe the vom off the stairs. Undress him – what does he do? – he pukes. I drag the sheets off of the bed. I don't wanna tell ya the rest. And ya think he got it outta his system, this whole – I wanna marry her – thing?'

'Let's hope so.' The bed looks comfier than the floor, but I'm not sitting on the bed for obvious reasons. I stand where I am, crunching my cheese on toast, feeling uncomfortable, and watch Axel make his big spliff, then decide I may as well sit after all.

'Be nice ta think so, huh?' Axel nods, pokes at his creation with a bit of rolled-up cardboard. 'Fact is, boy worse than ever. And now he got his self a plan. Try an win her back. Wanting his sibling ta help him too. Meanwhile, ya wanna help me with this?'

I shake my head, 'Did I wake you up?'

'Was I sleepin ya mean? I don't remember. One of them nights.' He grins like a schoolboy caught looking at grandma's underwear. 'Ooh,' he says, wincing. 'My goddam back.'

95

'What's up with it?'

'Kinda injured myself earlier. Draggin *Vomit Boy* up the stairs did not help me none neither. What he been eatin today, you got any idea?'

'Can I tell you something?' I say before he starts off on one of his marathon *me me me* sessions. 'I've had a bit of a problem. Something's... happened.'

'Go 'head. It aint the car? You not crash it, Sib, don't tell me you crash it?'

'No,' I smile, 'nothing that bad. I didn't crash it.' Imagine that. Would I do a thing like that? Would I be so stupid? Ha ha ha. Ho hum.

'So it broke? You had to leave it some place?'

'Not... *quite.*'

'Heck, not like it wouldn't serve his ass right. My back, *God*, you couldn't do me a big one here could you?'

'What's that?'

'Rub a little of that oil inta my back? It's ready mixed, it's no problem.' He nods towards the little cd cabinet in the corner. 'It's just on top there.'

'My hands are a bit cold.' Ha ha, don't scare me, please.

He lights up, moves the cushion so he's lying on his stomach, 'Ya sure yeh don't want ta try some a this?'

'I don't really smoke.'

'Eat some then. Relax ya. Y'lookin tense, Sib. Lookin more like it *you* need the massage. I'm achin here but ya the one with the tight muscles. I guarantee it. Here, let me feel those shoulders.' He puts down his joint for a moment and kneels behind me, rubs my shoulders through my black shirt, making me tenser than ever. 'Trust me,' he says like someone who should never be trusted.

'Right.'

'That feel good?'

'Yeah,' I lie through fiercely gritted teeth.

I have never felt tenser in my life. 'That's nice, I feel better now. Thanks.' In other words: stop now, *now*.

'Here,' he leaves off for a second, one hand still on my shoulder but the other leaning over into his drug box, pulling out a block of black resin. 'Take a bite a that, ya don't wanna smoke, that's tha thing ta do. It be cool.'

I do as I'm told, take a bite. What have I got to lose?

'Now ya sure you had enough there?' Axel looks at what's left, sounding slightly shocked, like he's torn between laughing at me and screaming at me. I crunch the smelly stuff in my mouth, biting into my cheese on toast in the hope that it'll take away the nasty flavour.

'Did I take too much?' crunch crunch.

'No, no, you cool.' His hands back massaging - or just *annoying* - my shoulders again. 'Your bro, Theo, last words before he die tonight. He kinda die earlier but then wake up with a little bit a lucidity. Wanted me to have a word with his Sib.'

'What did he want?' I have an excuse to turn round and look at him, forcing him to stop massaging me without having to directly scream in his face and tell him to fuck off.

'Want ya t'do something for him. You in-er-ested?'

'Have to tell me what it is first.'

97

Axel gets up and goes back to his spliff, lies back on his bed inhaling and holding in smoke before exhaling little grey mushroom clouds into the air. He takes his time replying; I've got my toast, I don't mind. Though I am starting to feel a bit weird suddenly. A bit... weird. 'What it is, is this. His Ava she not talkin to him, 'kay?'

I nod. Whooze whooze. 'We've established that.'

'So takin it to the next level in his mashed-up head. He goes, I been *unfaithful* to her. The only way I can get her back is if she fuck someone else. That the way he say it. She fuck someone else he back on a level playing field, his words.'

I can hear someone humming but it might just be a loose connection in my ear. 'But if she gets off with someone now she's not cheatin on him so it doesn't mean the same thing.'

I could eat his candles, I'm sure wax is very nourishing and filling. 'She's on the rebound, right?' I say. 'She's not goin out with him...' something something goldfish level of concentration '...besides, it's an absolute load of bollocks. I mean, isn't it?' I don't know but whatever he's saying is bound to be. I'm working the percentages. 99.87% of the time Axel is talking complete numskull codswallop. Why should now be any different? 'She's not goin out with him any more,' I say, but I think I've already said that.

He comes and sits down with me, pours oil into the palms of my hands, 'Nah but, Sib, ya rub me here for a second, yeah? There, there, yeah, on the money, yeah. Must be some trapped nerve thing, oh that's so much better... But Theo he a computer programmer, he trained to get the logic right. Here's how he want to play it, he sayin she still technically cheatin if she take it to the next level.'

'I don't think I'm getting any of this.' I am definitely feeling whoozy; he has stopped making any sort of sense.

'Some guy in a bar and it don't mean nothin, like you say it. So he lookin at me to be the guy. Thing is he don't like the idea of any actual *anything* happening, he more got the idea she *about* to do it. Thought crime. Look the guy sick in the fuckin head but you gotta play along with him, keep him happy. What ya gonna do?'

I smile as I start to take it in, Theo thinks that if his best mate gets off with the woman he loves-so-much-it-hurts it'll mean she's guilty and he'll become innocent again. You have to laugh. As if two plus two ever made less than seven and a haff when the love gods are doing their maths.

Axel says, 'But she know me so she aint gonna go for it and besides - hey, don't stop, I'm enjoying this, this is the best massage I had in a long time. What I sayin is, I aint normally so good with the sort of girls your Thee goes for.'

'What d'you mean?' I stop with my oily back scratching - this is news to me. I assumed Axel was even more Mr James Bond than my brother is. The fact that I never so much as seen him with a woman I credited to the way he wham-bam-thank-ya-mam dissed em two hours after the first date. I thought that was his style: no emotion, lots of pumping, lifting and sweating. Or was that some bizarre baby oil dream I once had...

'So what does he want me to do?' I almost shout.

'Theo think if it you that she get off with then that make her guilty again. It's his theory of relativity.'

'What?' Excuse me, that should be, 'WHAT!?'

'Hey hey, take it easy.'

I try and stand up, I try and leave, but my legs persuade me not to. 'What is he talking about? I mean, yeah, it'd be pretty deviant if she got off with a freak like me, but I think we can pretty much take it for granted that she wouldn't be interested. If she went out with Theo she's not gonna be interested in me or did he not work that one out? Is he crazy?'

Axel comes over, hands on my shoulders, giving me full on eye-to-eye contact. 'He's drunk, but listen, when he sober this still his idea. Y'say you owe him a favour. Right? So ya either does or ya don't?'

His car, the real love of his life. I nod pathetically. I think I'm going to be owing Theo a number of favours.

'Look, we know she not gonna go for ya. Not without our help. She not that kinda girl.'

'I could have told you that.'

'So we dress you up. Get ya lookin all smart and funky.'

'I think I'm gonna need a bit more than a clean vest and a pair of sandals.'

'Nah nah, it be fine, it be fun. Listen, Theo got more lines than the middle of the road. He help ya, you be fine.'

'Aren't you overlooking a big - a very *big* - problem here? To do with this girl finding me the tinsiest bit attractive?'

'Ya know what Theo say about ya? He call you an equal opportunities employer. Say you not care about sex, orientation, colour, creed or ugliness.'

'Are you sayin that I'm some kind of slut?'

'Hey, he say he only seen ya with three people, but they all different.'

'Well that's probably because there's only been three people, since... since, what has it got to do with you?' I'm getting ready to bite him.

Axel holds up his hands, 'Hey, I aint tryin ta get a down on ya here. I admire ya is all, if ya want tha truth. Open to new things an all that shit. Just your bro? He think he goin out on the edge cos Ava she not a blonde. That a big move for him. He be tryin ta persuade her to get it dyed, otherwise I can't see it happening long term anyways.'

'She isn't really his type, is she?'

'But I reckon by the way you say it, ya like her, huh, Sib?'

'She has certain qualities.' I don't know what to say. I don't know what I am saying, 'This is ridiculous. How can I - *I* - chat up and take his ex-girlfriend to bed? *Come on.* And even if *I did* - after she'd been to bed with me she'd hardly want to go back to Theo would she?'

'You're that good huh?'

Oh you sleazy sleazy man. I feel so tired and light-headed. I'm tempted to let him fuck me. As if I haven't been tempted since the first time I ever met him. If he wouldn't just spoil things by talking and being so stupid and haff-American. If he could just grin and dribble and be my dog. I pick up the cushion and throw it. 'Fetch,' I say like someone whose mind is starting to drift out of control.

'What ya say?'

'Yes,' I tell him. 'I'll do it tomorrow. No problem. She won't be able to resist.' I laugh and rest my head on his oily shoulder. Save me, save me. Wrap me in your arms and save me.

'I will,' he says like he can hear my thoughts. Like I'm speaking my thoughts and Axel he's holding my face in his hands and looking at me with those baby blue Kurt Kobain eyes.

'Good,' he says. 'Bad,' he says. 'Yes,' he says. 'No.' Kiss. Kiss kiss kiss. Kiss kiss.

Nine

Kiss kiss. Slobber slobber.

'Hey, wait a minute, what are you doing?'

That blonde hair and pointy chin, those bright eyes, the wetness he leaves behind after he's finished dribble-kissing my neck. It's like being woken up by an Afghan Hound.

'Hey, you're awake.'

'You mean you were kissing me while I was asleep? You didn't think it'd be polite to sort of ask me first?' I've got a bad head. I've got a very bad head and I can't move my bad head. I think someone has nailed me to the floor.

'Was just wakin you up,' he says, grinning, then puts his finger to his lips and whispers, 'thought it'd be fun.'

I listen. Thudding footsteps plonking about. It really is morning; that's baby brother's bear feet stomping to the bathroom. Brush his teeth, empty his bowels, have a shower. Takes fifteen minutes maximum by my reckoning. I wonder if I've left it too late to come up with a fantastically cunning plan.

'S'how ya feelin?' asks Axel. 'Want me to get you some juice?'

I shake my head. Too many questions, too many assumptions. I'm lying on the Hessian rug in the middle of Axel's dusty-red room, white sheets draped over me.

Errr.

Let me just check something.

I'm not naked.

I'm semi-naked.

Underwear intact.

Or.

Underwear back on.

Do I have any idea? Do I have any memory? I vaguely - no correction - I most certainly remember Axel's big wet dog-tongue slopping into my mouth and wrestling with my own drug-anaesthetised tongue. It seemed quite pleasant at the time. Quite comforting and relaxing. It took my mind off things.

I can't believe I let it happen. I can't believe it took me so long. I knew it'd happen from the first moment I saw him. I thought it'd never happen outside of some fevered unimaginative daydream:

I've been meaning to get fit, do you think you could help me workout? Ooh, sorry, I always exercise naked and covered in baby oil, is that a problem? ... etc etc etc.

He's getting dressed, in his own Axel summertime way. Shorts, vest, flip-flops, alice-band, watch. Giving me a brief flash of buttock but turning away to preserve my modesty.

I check again. Is there a reason why the label's on the outside?

'Tea, coffee, toast?' he asks like a sugar-voiced airhostess.

I sort of shake my head. Only sort of. The nails that are pinning me to the rug won't let me move any more than sort of.

The toilet flushes and the bathroom door squeaks open. Axel goes out and speaks to Theo. 'How you feelin this fine morning?'

I can only hear happy Axel, baby brother a faint hum, speaking in his usual early morning grumpy gnome voice.

'Yeah drove it back. No, no problems. Spoke last night. Key? Think I gotta bunch of em in my room, let me just check.'

Axel's voice getting louder. Like he wants me to hear.

Keys. The car. The car keys. Octavia. Beautiful wanton Octavia.

Fuck. Fuck me sideways.

I have no idea if he did. Though if he did it's the sort of thing I'd probably remember. I think I'd definitely be able to tell.

I think that probably gets rid of the doubt.

Outside the door they're chatting about last night. Cars, beer, women, vomit; I de-tune so all I hear is static.

I don't think we did. I don't know *what* we did, but if this was a game of baseball, nobody's scored a home run just yet. As far as I'm aware of the rules of baseball, we're still standing nervously at first base. Though someone might have tried to steal second while I wasn't looking. It's a chance you have to take when your brain and body aren't on speaking terms.

Brain to Bod: well, what's been goin on?

Bod: If you paid more attention and kept your so-called *wits* about you, you might have been there to find out.

Brain: Don't be such a sourpuss, did we or didn't we?

Body's giving nothing away; Brain hasn't got a clue. It's just, if we did, I would've liked to have been there. Body's a bit achy but that probably has more to do with the whole crashed-out-in-a-drugged-stupor-

105

on-flatmate's-cold-floor scenario than anything else.

We did kiss. He kissed me again this morning. Does that mean I'll have to speak to him all the time now, cos I think I might have to become a drug user on a regular basis if I'm going to have to put up with his inane chatter. If he just barked and gave me big wet kisses I wouldn't mind so much.

Outside bro is saying something about getting up late and having to rush, he slams back into his room and Axel returns.

'Keys?' he asks.

'What keys?' I say, sitting up, pulling the sheets around me.

'The car keys?'

'Oh. The car keys.' Really, I'd slap myself if I had the energy.

'He wants em, boy in a bit of a rush. Got meetings with clients an all that work shit.'

'Right,' I say. 'I'll just get them.'

I'll just jump out of the window and fly away to freedom would be a more sensible and realistic thing to say.

Theo knocks on the door; Axel puts his back against it to prevent any sudden interruptions. The look of terror on his face mirroring the one on mine. I feel like someone's just poured hot acid with a touch of chilli pepper into my brain. Axel whispers to me, 'I'm not sure I'm ready to like...'

He doesn't have to say it, I'm not sure if I'm ready to like... either.

'Don't let him in,' I say in a panicked whisper, jumping up and somehow managing to keep wrapped in my white sheet, overcome with ridiculously unnecessary morning-after modesty.

'Just a minute,' Axel looking at me like he wishes he hadn't. Like he's realising why he never did before. 'Tryin to remember which pocket I put em in.'

'Oh you've not lost them?' whines the little brat outside the door.

Axel turning back to me and mouthing, '*Give me the fuckin keys*,' as quietly but aggressively as he can.

'If only it were that simple,' I whisper back.

Theo turns the door handle and pushes, Axel's heavy body blocks him.

'What's goin on?' says Theo. 'Is this door locked?'

'Won't be a minute, don't rush me, man.' He looks at me, blue eyes as innocent as a baby's. 'Think Sib got em upstairs,' he says shaking his head.

'Why didn't you say that before?' Theo tutting and clodhopping up to my room, knocking again.

'What did you say that for?'

'Had to get rid of the guy. So where's the fuckin keys, what's goin on here?'

'I was tryin to tell you last night... but... the car got stolen.'

'*What?* Why the fuck didn't ya –'

I try and shush him, I try to explain. 'It's a long story. I know who borrowed it –'

'Borrowed it? You lent Octavia to some dude ya know? Or some dude ya don't know stole the motherfucker? Cos I don't know which is fuckin worse. And your brother don't know none of this shit, like eight hours later? That car could be in fuckin Brazil by now.'

Upstairs, Theo knocks again, says my name, tells me to wake up, calls me lazy then stops. Presumably now he's opened my door. He's checking under the rumpled duvet: a family of beavers and a small child, nothing more. He really should check the wardrobe, I always do. You never know what might be lurking inside.

'Ya gonna tell him now,' Axel shaking his head, walking towards me; I'm backing away towards the window.

The glass breaks - I sprout wings and fly away.

Is it really that impossible to imagine?

Theo comes thumping down the stairs.

'You've got to hide me,' I say

'What ya mean?'

'We don't want him finding me in here, do we? Me wrapped in a sheet at eight in the morning? What's he gonna think?'

We look at the wardrobe, the futon, and the tiny cd cabinet in the corner. Sometimes it pays to have the ability to fold up like a flat-pack self-assembly cupboard.

Theo knocks on the door. 'Not up there,' he says. 'Have you any idea what's goin on?'

'*No*,' says Axel, doing his best to sound innocent, 'might be up already. Down in the kitchen.'

'That strikes me as pretty unlikely.' Theo frog-marches his way across the landing and boots his way down the stairs.

'So,' says Axel. 'You got about ninety seconds. Explain.'

'I gave a ride home to my boss and his friend. And his friend. He wanted a go of the car.'

'He wanted a go? He wanted a *go* of the car? *What*?'

'Then. Then he drove off.'

'Oh this is bad. This is so fuckin bad. And ya aint seen nor heard from him since? Ya aint thought of fuckin calling the cops?'

I shake my head. I don't suppose crying'll get me any sympathy now. I don't know what to do.

The wardrobe looks so dark, well built and tempting.

Theo's clattering his way back up.

My heart and brainwaves have pretty much stopped. If I had ninety seconds before, I've pretty much decided to take it easy for the last fifteen. Theo doesn't knock; he comes straight in. I just have time to open the wardrobe door but not quite time to climb in. At least not completely. If only I'd had another fifteen seconds I would've had time to get my other leg in and close the door after me. Fact is, Theo's noticed. 'What's goin on?' he says.

I step back out of the wardrobe, trying to retain my dignity whilst wrapped in a sheet and with a head pounding like the death-drums of Valhalla. I don't know what they sound like exactly but I imagine it's quite bad. My head is quite bad.

'Just looking for clothes,' I say. 'You know what I'm like for doing my laundry, ha ha.'

Theo freezes, his brain's probably working as slow as mine is right now, so I'm in with a chance.

Axel says, 'This thing with Ava? Decided to get Sib sorted out with some clothes.'

'Axel said I could have a look in his wardrobe, but nothing really fits.'

'So why were you actually trying to climb in?'

'Looking for shoes.'

'Listen, you're weirding me out here. About the car –'

'I'm sorry,' I tell him. 'I don't know how it happened, it was a mistake. A sort of miscalculation.'

Theo's face is a picture, and surprisingly it's not Edvard Munch's *The Scream*. This picture is more like some gruesome laughing little sprite. I try and keep some Mona Lisa dignity, wrapped in my sheet, wondering if I say – *Look up there!* – and close the wardrobe door behind me they'll realise where I've gone.

'Errr.'

Axel says, 'Listen Theobald, we got a problem here and it ain't your Sib's fault, that's what you gotta remember.'

'Who's fault? What isn't? What are you telling me?'

'Last night. Sometimes you with a friend and things... things they just kinda get outta hand. They take advantage.'

'Sorry, I don't get it.' Theo's looking puzzled, dressed in his black suit, shirt and tie arrangement. Axel turns round to look at me; it seems it's my turn to speak. Or my turn to hide in the wardrobe or jump out the window.

'What's goin on with that sheet? If you want to borrow clothes why are you wrapped in a sheet? And d'you know what time it is? You never get up this early.' Theo, his face changing from executioner to jolly clown. 'Did you sleep in here? You look wrecked.'

'Had a little too much to eat, if you get my meaning,' Axel points at his drug box.

Theo can't help laughing. 'Passed out? You're

as bad as me. Guess you had your hands full last night then,' he says to Axel, shaking his head at the hilarity of it all. 'Anyway, I've gotta get goin. See ya all later.'

'Bye,' I say, gripping my white sheet with my white knuckles.

Theo looks at me, 'I wish I had my camera.' He laughs. 'Better get off then.' He goes to the door.

'Are you gonna get the bus?' I ask, for no reason. I have no reason to bring up the subject.

'No,' he says and goes, then comes back. 'And next time, don't just leave my car keys on the floor in the hall. Anyone could have trod on them. That's the way things get lost.'

'Okay. Sorry about that.'

Theo leaves the room; my heart starts beating again. It was all a dream. I'll wake up any minute with a big happy smile on my face. Certain aspects of the dream weren't that bad. I enjoyed the drugs and the kissing. Perhaps I should see if I really can fly before I wake up and realise I've wet the bed and I'm late for work.

Axel says, 'What the hell's goin on here? The car?'

'I don't know,' I say, truthfully, but obviously lying.

'You say a guy you know stole it?'

'Harry's friend, my boss Harry's friend.'

'Irish guy. But he bring it back right?'

I shrug, 'Someone did.'

'This between me and you. All this between me and you. Theo find out, I dead, you dead, I tellin ya.'

'Listen, last night... did we...?'

'Huh, what?' He smiles, sunglasses on his head

111

like he's ready to go out, hustling round looking for things, not giving me the full attention I deserve.

'How far did we...?'

'I kissed ya, y'kissed me back. Felt pretty good from this end. But if ya askin - did we? - then no, ya out of it pretty quick. Kind of like a disappointment. Like Sleeping Beauty in reverse. One kiss from me and ya out cold.'

'So if all we did was kiss, who undressed me, the clothes fairies?'

'Hey, with my back the way it is, ya think I gonna carry ya ass up them stairs? You rather wake up with your shoes on? Just tryin ta do the right thing here, Sib.'

'Do you have to call me that?'

'Ya don't like it? We have to think of somethin else to call ya.'

'You could always try my name.'

'Nah, don't think that's gonna work, ya Sib to me.' He's ready to go out to do whatever urban warrior activities he has to do today, his little backpack full of gubbins, his sandals and sunglasses on.

I nod and pick up my clothes - I'm borrowing the sheet – I'm out the door and zombie walking my way up to my room. Axel follows me out and locks his door behind him, but I'm too far up the stairs for him to kiss me goodbye. I don't know if I even like him. I don't like him being my brother's best friend, I know I don't like that.

I lie on the floor wrapped in my child-sized duvet and look in the tank at the pebble-pushers. Satan, Lorraine and Judas searching neurotically through the bits of stone for a stray flake of food they might have missed. The light's been on all night, they've had no sleep, and they probably feel as bad as I do. But Tankgirl's moved; that's got to be a good sign. I worry she'll die. Either of boredom or starvation. She doesn't seem to get on with the others; they've got nothing in common. They're busy all day foraging, mooching from one end of the tank to the other, from one end of the tank to the other, from one end of the tank to the other, from one end of the tank to the other, from one end of the tank to the other, from one end of the tank to the other, from one end of the tank to the other, from one end of the tank to the other. Tankgirl, she seems happy just sucking glass.

Baby Kurt comes over and looks at me. He shakes his head; he's disappointed, there's no doubt about it. Look at you, he seems to be saying, a common criminal and you could have been an astronaut.

'I'm scared of heights,' I say and sit up to get them some more food. Anything to keep them quiet.

'If only you'd had a bit more schooling,' says Baby Kurt, 'who knows what you could have been. Me, I'm just a beautiful silvery-white fish, if I had legs and a big fat brain... if I, if I, if...' but he's forgotten what he was going to say, flakes of fish and fish derivatives flaking down on his head.

Satan, Judas and Lorraine mob over, wagging their tails and darting round, trying to grab as much as they can. Even Kurt manages to forget about moral issues for a minute. They're like shoppers at the January sales; they don't care what it is, if it's on offer, they'll have it. I could be throwing in bits of cardboard or bits of fingernail; they'd still try and eat it.

'Listen, how about I buy you a little pirate ship to swim in and out of? How'd'you like that?' Satan and Lorraine look happy about the idea. Kurt looks at me like I'm stupid, he'd say something but he's too busy swallowing and digesting. He'd rather have a bit of urban desolation, a few Coke cans and razor blades, a crisp packet. He doesn't want some sub-aqua Disney treasure ship.

I huddle back under my duvet and stare at the fish in the tank, try and think, try not to think. Baby Kurt looking at me, not going away to pebble polish with the others. And all I can see are these bright serious eyes staring at me through the glass, asking questions without having to say a word.

Ten

'All I can see are these bright serious eyes staring at me, asking questions without having to say a word,' I tell Detective Harper.

'He never actually said a word to you? No? And then what happened?'

There's this thing where people who are lying start scratching their head, blinking, umm-ing, ahh-ing. I'm too scared to blink. My scalp's itching like a flea circus has moved into town and my brain's about as slow as the boy who sits at the front of the class with five pencils up his nose hoping to impress the girl that sits opposite. Today, I am *that* stupid and *that* dirty. I've not had a wash. I am not used to drug taking; I'm clean living. I might look like a shoplifting smackhead but my soul is middle-aged; I spend time thinking about fishtank ornaments and nail polish. I'd bite my nails but I'd end up with a mouth full of chipped black varnish, and I'm aware that that's not an attractive look, it doesn't impress police people.

'Errr, then? Then Harry comes out of his office because I said, umm, Harry come here, and err Harry says, here's the money, and passes the person the money. Then Harry unlocks the door and lets them out of the shop.'

'Them?'

'The person that was robbing us.' Smile nervously, shrug, honest open hands spread out: that's all folks. At the time, five minutes later, that was as far as the truth went, of course by now I should be adding a little *however... And then... By coincidence.*

This is my chance. A clean breast/a fresh start/a

coming clean. I bite my nails, I think I need to go on holiday. I think I need to not work here any more. Baby Kurt was right, everything ends unhappily, it's just the way things are.

I have no idea what Detective Harper and Detective Call-me-Jill are thinking. If they're students of body language; if they suspect it might be an inside job. I ask them if they want a cup of tea – I don't care if they're thirsty or not, I just want to escape. I go into Harry's office and put the kettle on and stand there waiting for it to boil, shout through and take orders for strength, sugar and milk.

I was late, I overslept, they were waiting for me when I got here. There was a bit of a hoop-la about me going home early last night and not staying behind to make a statement. Harry explained it all. He blamed himself. There's nothing they can do about it now. The police people just think it might have been a bad thing for me to go home like that, memory-wise. I assured them I could remember everything like it was yesterday.

I go back and hand the mugs to the relevant people, acting as confident as I can. Though I am allowed, strictly speaking, to be ever so slightly freaked out by yesterday's events. Yesterday's events up to the point where I got a taxi home from work. From there on in it was an enjoyable stress-free evening.

They're both making notes but Harper's doing most of the talking. Which suggests that he's the boss. Which tends to make me think Call-me-Jill is the clever one, watching like a cat while he growls his obvious questions at me again and again in the hope

I'll slip up, but not expecting me to say anything of interest, not acting like he's in the least bit interested in anything I have to say. But then it's like when you get your pushbike nicked; the police like to give the impression they've given up before they've even started looking. I suppose because if you do have your bike robbed, they never *are* going to actually start looking. If there's no tv cameras or a chance of promotion they probably think *what's the bloody point?*

He's bald like Harry, the man detective, a friar-tuck fringe of hair cut crisply round the back and sides. But he's got a moustache, so that makes up for it. Call-me-Jill, she's got a lovely glossy head of hair, cut schoolteacher straight; rimless glasses, mouth like a coin-slot, plain clothes. They both wear plain clothes, but then that's sort of in the job description.

Detective Harper, he says to me, 'As a result of there not being any cctv footage.' He stops, waits for me to nod. I wasn't aware there'd been a question but I nod. 'We're in a bit of a trouble situation in regard of identification.' I nod: I'm still awake, honest. 'All you can give us, as you say, is in terms of height, build, eyes, clothes and not a great deal else is there?'

I nod, 'No.' Then shake my head, 'Yes, that's right.'

'If you can just bear with me while I take a look at our notes. As I say, fingerprints are unlikely to get us very far with this being a public place that people come into... Let me just run it back at you, if you could confirm as I go through. Height – medium.'

Nodding dog.

'Build – slim to medium.'

'Uh huh.'

'Eyes... Now here you've changed your mind. Bluey-green or brown. We do know he's Caucasian. Unless, as you suggest he was wearing pale make-up and coloured contact lenses, and as you pointed out, as he didn't say anything he could have been female. But I think given the other evidence we've had we'll probably want to leave that idea to one side... Clothes again.'

'A jacket. A black jacket. Balaclava.'

'I thought you said it was a ski-mask?'

'What's the difference?'

'Well it's worth looking into, isn't it?'

'Errr, trousers, errr.' I don't want to lie, but I don't want to be the one that drops him in the chip pan fire. 'Training shoes.'

'Which you say were white.'

'Lots of people wear white trainers though don't they?'

'But it might be interesting.' Detective Harper chews his lip, scratches his tongue on his big man's moustache.

Harry starts asking about when we might be able to open again, Call-me-Jill tells him just as soon as the fingerprint people have finished doing their business. Shouldn't be much after lunchtime. Harry complains but I don't know why. I don't want to work here ever again. She reminds Harry that he really should get the cctv sorted out. Harry says he'll speak to Mr Hughie Jones, the owner, as soon as he can. First thing. In a minute. Get something sorted out. Harry says the insurance are coming round, that's the next thing.

'There's been a spate of robberies of this nature in this area,' says Harper. 'We think there's a gang involved. It seems to be highly organised.'

I almost burst out laughing. I can't help smiling. So highly organised they don't bother to check what's in their swag bag before they leave the shop. It's when I'm trying to hide my stupid grinning face that I notice Call-me-Jill, the quiet one, the nice one, the school teacher with the coin-slot mouth, is staring right at me. And not staring at me in a nice way, not complimenting me on the way my hair's all sticky-uppy, my eyes are bloodshot and the way I've managed to get black nail varnish all over my teeth. She's staring at me like a digital cctv camera. She's taking it all in and giving nothing away. And of course I am immediately convinced that she knows, she suspects or she thinks. That I've got a massive drug habit, four kids and a loanshark wanting to kill me. If she can find a motive she'll pin it on me. So that's where I'm in the clear, I've got no motive, no reason. I stare back at her, feeling suddenly confident, until she looks away and picks up her notepad, gets ready to go. 'You'll be available to contact on your home number outside of office hours?'

'Yes, yes.' Smile, smile. Eye contact, honesty, no fear.

'We're thinking we might have one or two leads that might be worth following up, so you'll have to stay tuned.'

'Ha ha, yes, good luck.' Where's the nearest travel agent. One-way ticket to Honolulu, please.

When the detectives have gone, the fingerprint people still on their hands and knees making a powdery mess of all the door handles, I say to Harry, 'I'm surprised they're bothering to check. For fingerprints I mean. It's not like they're going to know which fingerprints belong to the robber. This place must be full of grubby thumbprints.'

'You're not wrong there, Sunshine. No, I don't think this little bit of investigation has a great deal to do with our particular robbery. *Po*lice just reckon on how a place like this is full of petty criminals. People that've jumped bail, that sort of thing. They'll just take their prints back to the station and see if anything matches up. If it does you might find a few plain clothes people hangin round here over the next few days. Might have the odd arrest or two. These are gonna be interestin times.'

I smile and nod, a vision of normality for a split second before I relax back into the slough of despond. 'Harry, I don't want to work here ever again.'

'Course yeh do.'

'No, I've had enough, I can't cope with it.'

'What yeh gonna do for money, Sunshine? Yeh not got enough stashed away that yeh can afford to retire, have yeh?'

Errr.

Errr.

'No.' Smile, laugh.

The phone rings and I go into the office to get it. 'Hughie Jones bookmakers, how can I help you?' We don't do telephone bets. We don't do Internet bets, we don't do credit, we don't accept either Bulgarian or Monopoly money. It's either Harry's Mum, in which

120

case I won't be able to understand a word or...

'Hi Mum.'

'How are things?'

'Good, good, how are you?' Upbeat, don't worry, happy happy nightmare.

'Driving. Not so bad,' crackle crackle mobile phone. 'Anyway, we're on our way.'

'What do you mean?'

'Won't be long now. Your Dad says. Your Dad says half an hour but I'm thinking we might stop off at that new shopping centre and have a look round, seeing as we're passing. You don't mind, do you?'

'No. No, of course not.' I've just been in extreme danger. Guns, cars, wardrobes, family of beavers. No you take your bloody time why don't you.

'Then you can tell me all about it.'

Sex with flatmate, drugs, unhealthy eating habits, Paddington Bear's arse stuffed with fivers.

'Sure, sure, take your time, I'm not going anywhere.' Until I find my passport and a new adoptive parent for my fish. I can't very well go on the lam with them in a plastic bag like I've just won them at the fair. And how would Tankgirl cope? She'd have nothing to suck against. She'd probably just attach herself to Baby Kurt's dorsal fins. But then he could take it, in his usual miserable way. 'These things happen,' he'd say. 'Life sucks.'

Blah blah journey down, pots of tea in service stations, the price of a bag of crisps. 'We'll let you know when we're getting there and you can give us directions, save us having to work it out with a map. Bye then. Better not keep you from your work.'

Harry says, 'I've had the okay off the *po*lice fellas to open the place up again. Will yeh be alright on your own most of the day only I've a hell of a lotta things to clear up, as you can imagine. The insurance people for one.'

'Harry, I want to leave.'

'Yeh only just got here. Yeh can't leave, Sunshine, don't be silly. It'll be dinner-time soon and then we'll have a rush on. It's a busy afternoon today is, lots of races.'

'Harry, I don't wanna work here any more.' My face is a picture. It's a picture of a small child holding a dismembered Paddington Bear. The child's got big weepy eyes and there's a big sloppy tear dripping down its rosy cheek.

'Yeh can't leave yeh job these days,' says Harry, putting a sympathetic arm on my shoulder for a second then thinking better of it. 'Not with this government, yeh have to have another job to go to. The social won't give yeh no money.'

'Can't you sack me?' Sniffle sniffle.

Harry bright and upbeat, like he's explaining why my pet hamster had to die and why it's a good thing in the long run, 'You're too valuable to lose, Sunshine. All the training I've given you! Too highly qualified you are.' He grins and I can't help myself either. It's all just too ridiculous – I know that – but I can't help glowing slightly with pride. It's nice to be fantastically brilliant at your job. Even if your job does amount to not much more than adding up and taking away.

'I couldn't find a better employee. And after all

d'yeh not think it's not really a proper time for yeh to be leaving. What with the *po*lice investigating.'

'Meaning?'

'They'll be needing to speak to yeh again. They made that pretty obvious. Yeh can't run away.'

'What d'you mean?'

'From the difficult occasions in your life. Yeh have to be brave and face them. Or yeh'll be running all your life.'

'Oh.' That's a point. What am I actually gonna do when I arrive in Honolulu? What do I know anything about? If they race fish over there I'll be sorted. Look at the pectoral fins on that. $50 on the Siamese Tigerfish. To win.

'I'm opening now anyway so yeh'll just have to cope best yeh can.' I get the message; grit your teeth, no need to smile. If I smile in here they'll know I'm guilty. Everyone in here looks worried. Win and they're manic, lose and they're depressed; so most of the time everyone's just run-of-the-mill depressed.

Harry goes through and opens the door; the despond tribe comes flooding in. You'd think they had nothing better to do.

So the morning goes as mornings go. Except for the fact that I am in an acute state of fear and terror. Everyone knows the story by now. People whisper and look sideways like I won't notice. They even point at me through the glass. The glass that's supposed to protect me but is starting to make me feel like I'm in a zoo. It's not the first time I've felt like I was in a zoo or shop window but on those previous occasions...

'Mummy, I feel like I'm in a zoo.'

'You are dear, come along, let's go and see if we can feed the elephants.'

'Mummy, I feel like I'm in a shop window.'

'Will you come out of there. You're getting your mucky feet all over that nice material. And mind that train set you clumsy little oaf. Can't take you anywhere can we?'

I actually was.

Then it happens, it has to happen. I'm waiting, I'm shaking; this is the moment I've been dreading all morning. My Mum arrives. She rang about five minutes ago so it's not exactly unexpected. What is unexpected is that the Welsh Clint Eastwood came in again and Harry went over to speak to him. Then Charlie Strange came in and he joined in the conversation. Charlie in the same clothes he always wears, not coming over for a chat, like he's got nothing to tell me about what happened between him and Octavia.

I'm trying to stop biting my nails as I seem to have scraped the last flakes of varnish off them and my teeth are probably looking as pretty as a picture right now.

'So,' my Mum says, 'this is you. Working!'

'Yeah. Me. Working.'

'Do you enjoy it?'

'It's not too bad. Pays the rent.'

'Wouldn't want to get stuck here though, would you? It's just a staging post.' In my career as a celebrity bookmaker's clerk.

'Harry says if I stick around another ten years I might get made assistant manager.'

'We can talk about that later,' says Mum in that I-don't-want-to-have-an-argument-now way of hers.

Mum with her curly perm and glasses, wearing her posh black trouser-suit because she's coming into town for once. Not the wellies and jogging suit she normally wears when she's pottering around the garden. It makes me think, as we exchange small talk, me answering questions through the glass, it makes me think this must be what it's like to be visited in a high-security prison. Oh well, another vision of the future. It makes me wonder - what I'd be like – where I'd be now – if I hadn't been dropped by the social services stork down the chimney of my Mum and Dad's house. What if I'd been found at the bus station by some itinerant circus people, destined to wander the earth for all eternity thanks to some hideous curse. Or just because they get bored easy, and the clowns are wanted by the police.

We all have an infinite series of possibilities at the point of sperm/egg fusion. Creamy nice person omelette or cracked egg genius. It's not like the choice is exactly ours at that stage. Your Dad's hairy legs, Mum's nervousness, Granny Fuddock's susceptibility to colds, the milkman's lactose intolerance. Or the other way around. Or not at all. Because with me, this Mum and that Dad sitting in his disabled-stickered car down the road, we don't share any genes. I'll never have permed hair and wear unfashionable glasses like my Mum; I'll hopefully never grow a moustache like my Dad's.

'It's not the nicest place,' Mum says. 'I can't say I

felt very safe walking about round here.'

I don't disagree, 'Do you want to get something to eat?'

'That'd be *lovely*. Could we go for a meal somewhere? Are there any nice restaurants round here? Or is that a silly question?'

'There's a shop across the road that sells sandwiches, but I owe them some money.'

'What?'

'It's only for a taxi I didn't pay for. Don't look at me like that.'

Mum looks at me with her serious face, the one she was probably wearing last night on the phone; the one she'll have on the minute we get out of here. She was planning on keeping her cool-and-modern-face on while she was in here, the one that says, *'I am tolerant of other people, no matter how strange, weird, dangerous and foreign they look. I do not judge.'*

'Well, it's a nice day,' she says. 'I'm sure we can find somewhere to sit. Have a natter,' she smiles. 'Perhaps we can even get your Dad out. Get him some fresh air. Watch the people going by. Must be a tree we can find to sit under.'

'You'll have to have a word with my boss, that's the only thing. He doesn't normally let me go for my dinner until later on.'

'Can't you have the afternoon off? I thought we could have a troop around together, do a bit of shopping.'

'Round here? This pretty much *is* the shop, apart from Abdul's across the road, but then you can buy anything you want in there. It's quite a shopping experience.'

I point her towards Harry, still talking to the Welsh Clint Eastwood in his paint-speckled white tracksuit and Charlie Strange in his beautiful skin and white trainers. Mum goes over to them, looking like the most confident person in the world: which she sometimes pretends to be.

Then we're out of there and across the road in Abdul's. There's me, there's Mum, there's Charlie Strange standing in the corner flicking through puzzle magazines.

'They do a good selection of sandwiches normally,' I say, taking Mum to the chiller-cabinet: pork pies, reduced-for-quick-sale pasties, three sandwiches, 'so long as you want cheese, tuna or beef.'

Now Charlie Strange is having a quick peruse of the gardening magazines.

'I'm not sure what your Dad'd want. Thinking I might get him the pasty.'

Now Charlie Strange is standing next to my Mum, picking up a carton of milk then putting it back down.

'How about corned beef?' says my Mum. 'Ages since we had that.'

'Wouldn't catch me eating beef,' I say, loud enough for everyone in the shop to hear, picking the cheese'n'pickle sarnie. 'Don't know where it's been, do you?' Wouldn't catch me eating cheese normally either. Congealed fat and water lumped into a block and dyed yellow with a Frenchman's spit. But each to their own. Some people's spit you don't mind getting in your mouth.

Charlie plays it cool, wanders over to the greeting cards carousel like he's just remembered it wasn't milk he wanted, it was an anniversary card. But if he's trying to scare me pantless, it's having the required effect.

'Let's get out of here,' I say, carrying the sandwiches and a carton of banana milkshake over to the till. Mum tells me she wants to pay, but I pull out another fifty pound note and tell her to put her money away. It's not the cleverest thing I could do in the circumstances: showing off how rich I am. Not when Charlie Strange is hanging round near the till trying to make up his mind which penny chew to buy: but it feels good. It makes me feel like a successful businessperson for a second. Then a second later I get the usual foreboding and a third second after that, I wonder if I'm going to be spending all my ill-gotten gains on taxis and sandwiches. Criminal life doesn't seem so great when all you get out of it is a lift home and a selection of ready meals.

'Your boss said he didn't mind if you took a bit longer than normal for your lunch. He said he'd understand.'

We walk over to where Dad's little red car is parked and I wave and smile. I'm embarrassed talking to him sometimes, once we get going, arguing about third-world debt and dental hygiene we're okay. But I've not seen him for a while and the last thing we spoke about – apart from my career and my appearance – strangely we never talk about his laughable taste in cardigans – the last thing we talked about was the number of beggers on the streets these days. He thinks it's a good thing. I don't.

Dad: 'If people are stupid enough to give them money, I don't blame them begging.'

'Dad, it doesn't work like that.'

'It's a career path they've chosen. With a good hourly rate I would think.'

'But not enough to buy them somewhere to live.'

On and on until we get down to the, 'You bleepin idiot.'

'What do you bleepin know about it?'

Lots of huffing, puffing, gritting of teeth and going to bed angry. Angry silences the next morning. Angry lift to the train station, angry have a nice time, angry thanks for the lift.

So today I'm trying my best to be cheery.

'Hi, Dad, how are you?'

'Good, very good, how are you?'

'Not too bad.'

'Good,' cough. 'Good, good.'

Mum gets in the back and I get in next to her.

Dad doesn't say much when he's not having one of his big debates. He didn't say much before the accident; he's got even less to say now. He got run over by a fork-lift truck. It shouldn't sound funny and it doesn't sound funny, but it is a pathetic, tragic thing to happen. You expect fork-lift trucks to run over your toe or your sandwiches, not leave you in a wheelchair. He got compensation but there is no compensation as he'll be the first to tell you. He sits there all day listening to the radio: pop music of the 70s and people arguing about whatever the issue of the day is. Whatever it is, they disagree with it and Dad agrees with them. It makes him very angry, but it's an anger he can enjoy.

Dad takes his time doing his indicate, mirror, manouvre, then carefully pulls out, doing everything properly and at a sensible speed. I give directions. I'm taking them home for a decent cup of tea. Then we're there and I go ahead to prop open the door for Dad's wheelchair and 3467 the alarm. I don't want any panic with Mum when I open the door and she hears the alarm going off. I stand on the doorstep, patting my pockets, checking for my keys. Then I see Axel's shadow moving around in the hall. I knock and in a second he's there, wrenching the door open.

'Come in,' he says. The door to Sheena's ground floor room is open. The mountain bikes have gone from their usual place in the hall. I follow Axel into Sheena's room and it isn't worth saying, it's so bloody obvious,

'We've been robbed. This is all my fault.'

Eleven

'This is all your fault? What you mean: *this is all my fault?*' Axel with a more than serious look on his face.

'I don't know. I'm sorry.' I want to cry.

'Hey, hey, don't blame yourself.' He hugs me; I let him. Then he stops, 'This *isn't* your fault, is it?'

I shake my head and move away.

Axel goes on, 'I leave the house for like two and a haff hours and this... How they know there no one in? And the alarm is always on. You did put it on, Sib? Cos it sure is switched off now'

'Yeah, course I did,' I answer, getting angry. 'I always switch it on.' I probably did. I probably might have. My head at the moment, scatter-brained, messed-up. Sheena's room, drawers emptied, clothes scattered, bed upturned, cds and creams and perfumes and magazines and tampons everywhere. It looks more like a modern art installation than a habitable abode for a successful young executive like our Sheena. And after this Sheena's gonna need more than a hug; she's gonna need class-A drugs or intensive psychotherapy if she's gonna cope with this sort of invasion. If someone did something like this to my room...

What am I thinking? Of course someone did something like this to my room.

'What about the rest of the house?'

'Same fuckin story,' says Axel. 'An it aint like they just taken all the valuable shit, that you could fuckin understand. This like they taken the valuable shit then left the door open for some fuckin junkie scum to come in and have fun rippin your house apart. It's fucked

131

up, Sib. Sheena's gonna shit. Like literally.'

Everything thrown and squeezed and splurted across the room. Broken bottles of perfume, her mirror squeezed full of face cream. I don't understand what their point was - that they were pissed off about something. Life, or something more specific. Of course I know. I just don't know what Sheena's got to do with anything, except she's in the way. Except they didn't find what they wanted and her room's on the way out.

'This room the worst,' says Axel. 'Our rooms it just like they lookin for stuff, down here it like they gettin angry an they breakin shit for fun. I tell you, this some fuckin twisted fucked up shit. Make me wanna fuckin kill someone.' He's shouting now. 'Looka tha door,' he points over. 'Got in tha house okay. How the fuck, I do *not* know. Like, they got a *key?* That one thing I'm thinkin about.'

Yes, Axel, and I'm way ahead of you on that one. That thought has occurred to me.

'Smashed open this door, did the same on mine. Couldn't get in ta Thee's room. He got too many deadlocks protecting his computers and porn collection an shit.' Axel almost smiles; I almost make a sarcastic comment. He sighs, 'Right now I'm startin to have some serious fuckin issues about livin in this area of town. Startin ta realise why it so cheap to buy houses round here.'

'It could have been worse I suppose,' I say like some old lady at a bus stop talking about something she knows nothing about. Talking for the sake of talking.

'Worse? Yeah, they could kill us in our beds and fuckin rape us an shit. Yeah it could be worse... I'm getting me a gun, aint no other thought on my mind right now, Sib. Next time some sucker breakin in to *my* fuckin English castle, they gonna find one fuckin *prepared* motherfucker.' He grins, like really he has to, the *Fantasy Island* self-deluding little fuckface. 'Hey, an cops are on their way, so, just so y'know, don't touch nothing till they dusted for prints. That's what they tell ya.'

'Yeah, I'm gettin kind of experienced at this now.' I half smile and pat him on the arm. I'm not sure I'm prepared to hug him again right now, not with my Mum waiting outside in the car. I need to go up to my room; I'm dreading going up to my room.

'Listen, Sib, what yo tellin me last night, about Thee's car? This guy takin it, *borrowin* it? Then this mornin it back, and me and you we don't say nothin? So ya gonna tell me? Like what the *fuck* was that all about? Cos the way *I* see it? Guy takes a bunch a Theo's keys when he take the car, alright? He play with her, ride her all night. I don't know how far he go or where he go but he bring it back here, cos he not a thief, he a friend of yours. And next morning? This. It's like, like he still got the house key, Sib. He did not have to break in. Y'didn't tell him the alarm number just to kick that outta the game too, huh?'

'You don't know if any of this is –'

'Oh, an ya got a better solution? Brighter ideas, cos I wanna hear em.'

'It could be a coincidence. People get robbed all the time.'

'Alright, point accepted. So, when y'left for work this morning, ya put the alarm on?'

'I think so, yeah.'

'Think so.'

'Why is this all about me all of a sudden?'

'Why is this all about *you?* Why d'*ya* think, Sib? Work it out.'

He is making me so angry with his smug landlord's face. I could hit him if he wasn't so much bigger than me and so bloody right about everything. It is all about me, there *is* no point in denying it. To myself. I'll deny it to everyone else though. But Axel better not try and start kissing me again with his big wet dog-lips any time this millennium.

'But then if that the case,' Axel still going on, like Mr fuckin Sherlock Homeboy, 'why he not have copies of the keys to Theo's room? They all on the same bunch. Why they have to try and kick that door in? And your room, that door, that aint kicked in, but then I guess ya forgot to lock it, huh?'

I forgot to put the alarm on, I forgot to bring my brother's car home, I forgot to kick you in the balls last night when I had the chance. I'm more forgetful than your average goldfish these days.

'I should go and have a look at my room. I'll try and talk about it with you later. Can we... d'you think we can keep this idea to ourselves for the moment?'

'Knock knock, only me,' says my Mum from out on the doorstep. I never did wedge the door open and go back and give her a hand with Dad and his wheelchair. Mum still sounding bright and cheerful. She rings the doorbell then knocks. The minute she gets through that door she'll start crying. She knocks again. 'Anyone going to let me in or do I have to bash the door down.'

'Could you?' I look at Axel. 'I really can't deal with

her right now. I need to go upstairs and...' Axel nods, I run into the hall and scoot up the stairs. I want to see what's happened before my Mum comes in and starts stealing my misery off me.

Up past Axel's room, having a quick look in: drawers ripped out and turned upside down, futon tipped up, the door kicked in; but compared to Sheena's... Then there's our Theo's battered but still triple-locked door... I go up the stairs to the top of the house.

My door hasn't been kicked in. Axel's right, I probably forgot to lock it. Though I always lock it, I lock it obsessively. They had the key, who am I trying to kid. I was wrong when I said I wouldn't notice if someone came in and robbed me. And they still didn't take those cups down; they didn't empty the bin for me. They smashed them; they emptied it. I start to feel momentarily lucky that they didn't defecate on the walls, though I haven't checked in the wardrobe yet.

My fish. What am I thinking? No, please. This is my nightmare. This truly is my nightmare.

Satan and Lorraine and Judas and Baby Kurt. Missing. Gone. Baby Kurt and all the others — all the others except Tankgirl. What have they done with them? Now I really am frantic, now I really am angry and sick and crazy with worry and fear. They didn't kill them and fry them and cover them in ketchup, please tell me they didn't. The big empty tank, the suckerfish girl superglued to the glass, looking somewhere with her sideways eyes but thinking about the joys of algae.

So I'm picking up my duvet and throwing it,

kicking books, clothes, socks, bricabrac and empty crisp packets out of the way. I'm expecting to see a little corpse somewhere. I'm hoping I'm not too late, that all the spirit and hope of those little fish is still hanging on somewhere. Please let there be a God, so it'll be worth my while suddenly deciding to believe in *him*. Or *her*. I don't really want to get into a gender discussion with my Godhead I just want my baby fish back. I run and check in my underwear drawer, tipped upside down. There's nothing, there's mess everywhere. The window's been wrenched open. They could have thrown them, given them the experience of flight for a second before the final experience of getting their heads smacked open. I hang my head out of the open window then think better of it, remember what Harry said.

I have to not think these negative thoughts; there is a sensible logical conclusion to make. I must not hyperventilate. I know what's happened. My fish have been kidnapped.

The police were right after all; this is a sophisticated thief who knows exactly what he's doing. I'll pay the money gladly just give me back my babies. I slump to my knees and look at the big empty tank. I didn't buy them a sunken treasure ship in all the time I had them. I didn't care for them properly. Tankgirl, tell me, am I a bad parent? I know you're welded to the glass, but you're not exactly the hardest to catch, are you? Tankgirl, tell me what happened, where's Baby Kurt?

I'm expecting to get a bit of fin in the post with a note attached. A Polaroid of Satan and Lorraine circling mindlessly in a tiny bowl. Blindfolded and forced to exist on an oatmeal diet.

I can't help thinking this was more than one person, it's just too much destruction for one person to perpetrate.

Downstairs I can hear Mum's squeals of dismay, Axel's words of reassurance. It's like she's the one that's been robbed and abused. Axel's shouting my name, but I'm not going down there. I tell him to come up. I'll tell him everything, or a portion of everything. I hear the footsteps coming up the stairs, the intake of breath at the mess that is my room, my life,

'It's my fault. I'll make everything better. I know who did it. And now they've kidnapped my fish.'

'Oh dear, isn't this awful,' says Mum. 'I can hardly believe it.' She's bawling her eyes out. She probably would have cried if she'd seen my room before the robbery never mind now.

'Come here.' Now Mum wants to hug me, seems I'm just so huggable these days.

'I'm sorry, I'm sorry.' I can't help joining in with the weeping and wailing. It seems so necessary. 'I know that it's all my fault.'

'Hey, don't be silly. It's nobody's fault, a thing like this.'

'They've kidnapped my fish,' I say though I know she's not going to understand or care.

'Kidnapped your what?' She looks at me with a puzzled face, like someone trying to decipher a Seeing-I picture. *Let me get this straight.* 'Who has?'

'I've got to go.' I've got to go and check in the back garden. See if they've been thrown out the window.

'Where are you going?'

137

'I'm going to find whoever did this, get my fish back and sort this out once and for all.' I'm going into the cellar to get Paddington Bear. But they don't get Paddington till I get Kurt Kobain and the rest back.

I run into Axel, on his way up, as I come bouncing down.

'Sib, what's happenin?'

I push past him. He carries on up, speaks to my Mum.

The front door's still wide open, Dad's in Sheena's room, but I don't want to talk to him either. Though a good bit of shouting and air-clearing might do me some good. I go to slam the front door shut behind me - but stop - because who do I see - standing over the other side of the road, just watching, just standing there. Looking as innocent as he ever could with those devil's eyes and cheap white trainers. I don't think about it, I don't have time to consider, I slam the door and storm across the road.

'I bet you think this is pretty funny, don't you?'

'And what might that be?' he says, his face all offended and innocent like a fox being accused of having an interest in chickens.

'My house getting robbed like this.'

'Oh that's very unfortunate for you. Two robberies in two days, you're not having a very good time of it, are you now?'

'And where are my fish?'

'What fish are they?'

'You know damn well. Where are Satan and Lorraine and Baby Kurt? Where are they?' I forgot to ask about Judas, but he's never been my favourite. I really am a bad parent.

'Fish? If you want fish there's a chip shop down the road, I'm sure they could give you a couple of fish if you ask them nicely.' He looks at me with those magician's eyes. 'If you've got the money to pay for them.'

'You must be out of your mind,' I'm pointing and shouting. I'd be hitting him, but I'm not completely insane. Axel's coming, rushing out of the house; a police car is cruising down the road towards us. 'If you think I'm gonna give you any money you've got another thing coming.'

Axel stands right behind me; he must have an idea what's going on here.

Charlie Strange starts to move off. 'I'm just walking past, y'know,' he tells Axel, like he's looking at Axel's muscles and assuming he's tougher than he actually is. 'And this one starts mouthing off at me. I'm on the way to the shop. That's all I'm doin. Talkin of fish, I might buy myself a little tin of pilchards. Quite fancy the idea of having myself a little fish and tomato sandwich.' He walks away, his face so smug I want to punch him and drown him in ketchup; then see how he likes being put between two slices of bread and having his head bit off. I grab him by the wrist, and he turns round looking truly startled, he wasn't expecting this.

'I'll see you at The Demented Squirrel at half past eight tonight.'

'The Demented Squirrel?'

'The Angry Squirrel. The pub you go in.'

'Ohh.' Happy little face. Yes, Charlie Strange, I give in, you get what you want. 'The Trusted Squirrel. Why? Are we going for a drink, are we? That'll be nice.'

'Don't play games with me, I'm fed up with it – and bring Satan with you.'

'*Satan*?'

'And Kurt and Lorraine and Judas. The *fish!*'

'Well I'd love to meet you for a drink later but I've no idea whatsoever what you're talkin about now.' He laughs and sparkles those eyes at me and for a second it feels like he really does want to meet me purely out of lust for my body and the draw of my vibrant personality. I let him go – go to buy his pilchards in fuckin tomato sauce.

Axel's kept out of it until now. 'What the hell's goin on, Sib? Seriously here? He the guy that took Octavia for a ride last night? Cos we got cops arriving from all directions, you want me to have a word?'

The uniform police are getting out of their car, going towards our house but looking across at us. I smile and punch Axel gently on the shoulder, so I'm looking upbeat and unworried, I hiss through my teeth. 'Let's keep this between me and you, agreed?'

I need to go and check amongst the weeds in the back garden. It could have been kids; it could have been vandals with no intent or purpose in their mind but reckless mischief. I'll find out more when I meet Charlie Strange tonight in the pub. Perhaps I have got this all completely *completely* wrong.

Twelve

No, I've got this all completely *completely* right. And that's why I have to run round and check the back garden, start stomping through the undergrowth, trying to work out any possible flight path, feeling all Galileo – if a fish were dropped from a certain height – making myself shiver inside when I consider the idea. It's easy to be flippant, it's harder to admit you care so much it makes you want to bleed.

There's no sign of anything out here, just itchy long grass, nettles and discarded house bricks. It's like looking for a goldfish in a haystack. So I give up, go back inside. I know this is wrong. I know where my fish are: in a darkened room, in solitary confinement, in a row of teacups on a shelf, barely alive. I'll get them back tonight. At £1000 per fish, it's not a bad deal as far as Mr Armed Robber in the white trainers is concerned. He must be laughing all the way to the bank, then getting his gun out and threatening to kidnap the clerk's puppies and kittens if they don't give him what he wants.

Then later when the police have been and gone - no detectives so far, just uniforms – Theo calls back, he's picked up his voicemail and heard Axel's message, he wants to know what's going on. I give him the general version, the official outline, of events. He tells me how pissed off he is but sounds pretty hoop-la when I tell him they couldn't get into his room. Then he tells me he'd like to chat but he's in a real important meeting right now, so he'd better cut it short.

Sheena came back as soon as she heard. She said she was in tears as she drove down the motorway. She was in even more tears when she came in and saw the policewoman standing in the middle of her tornado-blasted room. Now Mum's sitting with her on her metal-framed squeaky bed, arms round her giving her as much comfort as she can. It's like her boyfriend's an astronaut and we've just found out that his spaceship's exploded. Nobody knows what to say to her, no one seems to be able to help. We answered the police questions as vaguely as we could and apparently we're gonna start the tidying up process in a minute. Mum's taken complete and total charge. Dad's already wheeling round in his sleek new indoor chair, sorting things out in the kitchen. We're all on a war footing: the war on dirt and disorder.

Me, for once I don't care, I'm just ticking off the hours till eight this evening. That's when I get my life back. That's when this nightmare is over. I phoned Harry to give him the bad news about the burglary, but he didn't seem overly surprised. He did say he was sorry for me, he said I must be feeling very unlucky. Now there's a guy fitting a new lock on the front door and there's someone coming round as soon as poss to fit new doors for Sheena and Axel. Axel's standing in the hall talking on his mobile, getting whoever-it-is-on-the-other-end-of-the-line to agree to do something-something tonight. Axel wheedling and whining, cajoling and conniving. It doesn't surprise me. He told me that was the reason he had to go out this morning. He's setting up something special, something to do with our Theo and this girl he's so madly in love with. Axel and Theo's computer-brained plan to win her back through a process of mutual infidelity.

I'm going to go up to my room in a minute, as soon as I've paid my respects to Sheena, proved that I care enough to stand there and tell her she must be feeling awful. Then I'll go and vac up and sort out my laundry, and generally tidy up and throw away. I'm lucky in a sense, because it really would have taken a bomb to hit the place to get me to do such an intensive spring cleaning operation. And I'm lucky again in that I've not exactly got a lot of possessions in the first place, so there wasn't much to steal and there isn't much to clean. They didn't take anything inanimate from my room. Axel and Sheena, between them they lost: a cd player, a nicam vcr, a satellite tv digibox, a mini-disc player, a laptop computer, a rusting old mountain bike and a whizz-bang new one, aftershave, a large block of cannabis resin (not listed in official police reports), silk underwear, credit cards, loose change and notes. All they forgot to take of value were the cuddly toys in the cellar.

I lost my fish.

I went down into the cellar to check on Paddington Bear. They probably didn't even know we had a cellar, and even if they had they never would have thought to check on Paddington Bear's taped-up arse crack. He's sitting on my bed now in his duffel coat with the parcel tag round his neck, *Please Look After This Bear.* He's come all the way from darkest Peru in South America, in his big hat, his bear feet, hoping to get adopted by a nice family. Instead he gets me, wanted by dangerous people for my part in a botched-armed robbery.

It's the *armed* part of the robbery I've got to remember when I start thinking about cunning plans to get Kurt back. Baby Kurt with a gun at his head, a gun pointed at him through the glass.

I'll get to The Poisoned Squirrel early and find Harry. I have to find out if he knows anything about this. If he doesn't then I've got nothing to lose, I can give him the money and ask him to pass it on. Then it's his problem. His problem, my fish.

If Harry does know what's going on. If Harry is part of this. Then I'll give him the money and he can tell me where my swimmers are. Or that's what I'm hoping. I'm hoping Harry is the brains behind the operation. If I have to speak to Charlie Strange and look into his evil beautiful green eyes... chances are he'll get the bear but I won't get the fish.

'How you feelin?' I ask Sheena.

'Okay,' she sniffles. Never again will she be the bright, open, lovely personality everyone says she is. She'll be more like me from now on: jaundiced, cynical, stylish and witty. Well, the first two anyway ... 'I canna sleep in here t'night,' she says. 'I feel so ... all on my *oown* down here.' She is actually weeping, her chest heaving, her jaw shivering; even I don't feel the need to make a sarcastic comment. But then I am blaming myself and feeling appropriately guilty. What more do they want me to do, tell them the truth?

'There, there,' says my Mum, like the best mum in the world, 'we wouldn't dream of letting you be all on your own. You can come and stay with us in a hotel. We were just going to phone up and sort it out. It'll be a nice break for you.' Dad comes wheeling in with a cup of tea and some biscuits. Sheena gets up and gives

144

him a kiss on the cheek, dribbling her tears onto his nose. Both of them smiling despite it all and I have to stop myself from feeling jealous and left out, but you can only take self-pity so far before it becomes a horrible disfiguring personality flaw. Besides, I can't help admiring her and wanting to be more like her: open, honest, good looking. And that's why I hate her, naturally. Theo's words about me being jealous start ringing in my ears.

'No, no, thanks an all that,' sniffle sniffle, 'it's no good. I canna stay in a hotel all me life,' wipes away tears. 'I wanna stay here, in this house. This is supposed to be my home,' whine whine. 'I'll bunk in with one of these lot,' she points at me, but I presume she means my brother. After all it wouldn't be the first time; whereas me and Sheena, we're not what you'd call bosom pals, we're barely on speaking terms most of the time. Sheena, she says to my Mum, 'And I dinna want either of yous off staying in some posh expensive hotel. I won't stand for that neither.'

'Well that's lovely,' says Mum. 'How about *we* cosy in down here in your room and you get yourself sorted out up in one of the other rooms. If we all stick together I can't see that we've anything to worry about.' Mum smiles with a force of brightness that you can't even start to fight. If she were born in earlier times people would be convinced she was a prophet. Though it'd be a prophet of Tidying Up and Putting On A Brave Face. Saint Of All She Dusts. 'Soon get this place ship-shape if we all muck in - plus you've got insurance, haven't you? Ooh, it'll be better than new by the time we've finished.' Everyone nods and smiles. I'm expecting someone to offer to make a cup of tea any minute and then start reminiscing about the war. Meanwhile I'm pretty notable by my useless silence and general useless uselessness. The problem is I'm just not well equipped for this sort of *genuine* situation, I can't help myself.

'So shall I phone Theo and tell him the good news?'

'What's that?'

'That you're gonna be sleeping with him tonight.'

Sheena, Sheena, there, there. Off she goes again, just when it looked like she'd put a plug in the eye fountains. Mum and Dad look at me like they want to tell me I'm still not too big for them to put me over their knee and give me a good thrashing. Not that they ever did. I can't claim I was a battered child, I can't claim that I ever had anything bad happen to me, until now.

'I was thinkin more of askin if I could stay with you,' Sheena says, looking up at me with a sad smile on her sad wet face. 'Yeh wouldna object would yeh?'

'What about the tv room, there's a big sofa in there.'

'What with burglars prowling round! No thanks!' She's laughing; at least I can make her laugh.

'My Mum and Dad'll only be next door if you stay in there.' Ha ha ha. Some hope, some help they'd be. Though Dad's very good at making a fried breakfast - providing the cooker's low enough for him to get to - and Mum'll always bring you a cup of tea first thing. So if there's a burglar, they might not be able to stop him, but they'll make sure he doesn't go running off on an empty stomach.

Mum says, 'What's the *matter with you?*'

'What d'ya mean?'

'Sheena's just asking you to do her a simple favour.'

'I'm startin ta think I must smell,' Sheena pouting, moments away from streaming tears again. 'Feelin like this is not a nice situation and I'm gettin rejected left, right and centre to add to it.'

'*I'm* not rejecting you! *Course* you can stay with me.' I smile and think, *great*, but I'm not sure if that's, *great*, as in, fuckin *great*, why did this have to happen? Or *great*, yippy-dee-doo-da, the lovely tit-tattooed Sheena wants to share a bed with me. But it's probably a combination of the two.

So now we're all tidying up and sorting out. As far as Mum's concerned, this is just what she wanted, an excuse to get out the scrubbing brush and clean this deviant pisshole of a place we call home. Perhaps she organised the robbery, after all the only other excuse she'd have to get us all at it like this would be a visit by the Queen. And that's probably going to be considerably harder to organise.

Axel comes up to my room where I'm using the dustpan and brush, the vacuum cleaner on duty elsewhere in the house.

'Sib, sorry to like have to talk to you about this right now. Seems a bit the wrong thing, but y'know, I was at it all this morning, organising. Talking to this Felice, y'know, Ava's best friend? Don't know if you remember? Fact is, we got you a party to go to tonight.'

'You *are* joking?'

'No, serious. Listen. Remember the favour for

Theo? All the shit with the car and I'm not even *gonna* mention all this fuckin trouble we got here.'

'Don't, because it's got nothing to do with me.'

'Well I'm pulling in that favour right now. And, speaking to your moms? Telling her how I takin you out, she want me to take Sheena. It's like last night was cheer up Theo night, tonight it's make-Sheena-happy-night.'

'What am I meant to do?'

'Come with me. We get you dressed; we get you lookin fine. Lookin... *appropriate.*' They say everyone has *one* area of their life where they're supremely confident that they're right. That they're the best, that no one can challenge their knowledge. With Axel, he's the Saint of Cool. He knows everything there is to know about looking *right.*

Then I remember, 'I've got an appointment, actually. I'm meeting someone at eight-thirty or a bit before,' at The Mordant Squirrel, I'm dropping off a bear-shaped package. I've decided it's pointless me going if I don't take the money. I'd only have to hand it over somewhere else. Somewhere more private where they could stab me in the gullet and chuck me in the sewer.

'Meetin with that guy?'

'Sort of...'

'You want me with you as back up?'

'No, I'll be okay on my own.'

'How about I drive you there, right? We wait outside, and I aint gonna ask what it all about. Some time maybe but not now. You come out and I take ya to the party straight after. Keep callin it a party. Is a party, but like a party in a club or a bar. I don't even know what you call these places.'

'You must be getting old, Axel.' He looks at me with his eyes; like he's a young mountain wolf seeing a biped for the first time, and looking more amused than impressed.

'This girl's birthday or something. She aint the important thing. Forgotten her name, Emma or Amy, it more of an excuse, y'know? Anyways, you heard of a place called *Mattress?* Supposed ta be good if you're inta that kinda thing.' I shake my head. I've not heard of anywhere where anyone might go out to. I've heard of Blackfin Corydoras and Catterick racetrack. The simple fact is I don't get out much. 'You'll enjoy it,' he tells me.

'Yeah.' If there ever *was* a half-hearted person, then that person is me, today. But I can't stay in tonight; I can't come straight home after I've been to The Wrinkled Squirrel, not with Mum and Dad here, not with the video and satellite stuff nicked. We'd have to sit down and have a proper real *conversation* all night long, or at least until bedtime at quarter-past-eleven, and how hellish would that be?

Axel tells me, 'I got one word. You owe our boy Thee a favour. The word is *car.* Octavia. My knowledge of what happened last night.'

'That's more than one word.'

'Yeah but it's words that mean you sayin yes to whatever I suggest.'

'It doesn't mean I'm gonna do *whatever* you say,' and I'm smiling for some sick and twisted, perverted reason.

'You're gonna do this and then we'll see.' Axel's eyes sparkling, his cheeky grin as half-excited, half-bashful as mine.

Mum appears in the doorway. 'How's it going up here?' she's got the vacuum cleaner with her, the snake draped over her shoulder. 'I hear you're going out?'

'I believe so.'

'Well get yourself in that bath then. I'll finish off in here.'

'It's okay, Mum, I can manage.'

'I won't ask a second time.'

So I'm taking a bath, my Mum's cleaning my room; I'm going to a party in an outfit someone else is choosing for me. Remind me how old I am again?

Thirteen

Six? Sixteen? Twenty-six? Mum and Dad want to have a word with me before I go. I feel like I'm all dressed up and going off for my first day at school. A teenager going on an embarrassing first date. I feel like it's my big first day at hat-making college and they want to get me to promise to work hard. Or maybe they're just going to wish me well and pop a few quid in my pocket so I can be generous and get the drinks in tonight. Needless to say, I've decided not to stick my hand up Paddington's arse and grab a final few quid to keep me going. I've still got about sixty quid left from the last time. If I'm giving it back I can't very well keep robbing it. Though if Harry's not involved, Mr Strange Armed Robber has no idea how much should be in there.

'Well! Look at you!' Mum aghast, Dad mouth open, rubbing his eyes like he's dreaming.

'What d'you think?' Axel's dressed me. He has ideas and they're strange and perverted ideas just as I'd hoped. I do a twirl, my hair in a greased back ponytail, flopping about like a pony's tail.

'I wouldn't have recognised you,' says Mum.

'That's the idea.'

'It's not fancy dress, is it?' says Dad.

'*No.*'

'Oh.'

The thing is, I'm wearing a suit, Axel's hired it especially for me but it's still a size or two too big. The sleeves are long enough to hide my hands. It makes me look like I'm a child in an adult's clothes. Dressing me up like this is supposed to make me more attractive to Ava. It's something she once said to Theo, something he remembered. I feel like a little child dressing up in my Daddy's clothes. I don't feel right, I feel disturbed by the image of me in the mirror. Particularly if I half close my eyes and chew a pen like I'm smoking a cigar, then I look like someone else completely. Someone who needs locking up maybe but definitely someone who isn't me. And I quite like it, I have to admit. Though it took Sheena ten minutes to stop laughing even after Axel had explained the whole charade to her. Then she kissed me on the cheek and said what a good sport I was. Then Axel told me how good I look, whispered to me about what he wants to do with me when we get back. That's another reason why I'm enjoying playing this game. Plus, once I offload my adopted bear I get my babies back. I don't know how I get my swimmers back, I just know I will, and though I'll end up having gained nothing at all from this particular *charade* – give or take the odd taxi and mozzarella meal - I'll have gained some sort of understanding and appreciation of what I had in the first place, however dumb and obvious that might sound.

'We said we wanted a quick chat,' says Dad, 'and I appreciate your friends are waiting.'

'They're drinking vodka and watching that stupid video camera prankster show on the telly.'

Mum and Dad nod. The don't do telly unless it's home improvement or gardening. And at the moment they've got something big to say but they don't know quite how to say it.

'I found this on your bed.' Mum found Paddington sitting on my bed. Which saves me going back upstairs to get it. 'He's got all that tape on him so I thought I could give him a proper sowing up and stick him in the washing machine. It looks like he's been living under a stone for the past ten years.'

'Oh, great, thanks.' I grab my bear a little too aggressively. 'It's nice of you to offer but I'm happy with him the way he is. Got a lot of good memories this bear.' None of which spring to mind immediately, but there must be some, other than yesterday and ripping him open and pulling out his stuffing.

'The thing is,' says Dad. 'We were wondering what's goin on in your life. We think we need to have a proper sit down talk.'

I don't know what's brought this on, but I'm prepared. I can handle it, I'm cool. 'I know you're disappointed in me and you're wondering what I'm going to do next with my life. I'm always keeping secrets from you, never tell you what I'm up to. Listen, Mum, Dad,' I hug Paddington to my chest with a big enormous smile on my face. Enormous for someone whose house has just been robbed, whose loved ones have just been kidnapped. 'Paddington was adopted and I was adopted and we both just get on with our lives, it's not a problem. I'm not even sure you get to a stage where you *decide* what you're gonna do with your life. I think a lot of people just live. And they're happy.' Blah blah blah blah.

'What we were trying say is,' Mum more serious than a maths teacher, 'we'd like you to feel you can tell us everything. No matter what. We want you to know that we won't judge you. If there's something going on... in your life... that's a bit... *fishy* –'

'What?' I'm actually cocking my head to one side

like a confused dog. '*Fishy?*'

Dad butts in, 'We don't know what it is, we don't *care* what it is. If it's drugs that you're into – we can understand that – but whatever it is – we'd like you to tell us, so we can try and understand and help as best we can...'

'Where's all this come from? What d'you think I am? A drug dealer? I'm sorry, I don't know what you're talking about.' I have to laugh, but of course, just as suddenly as I was happy, I'm now incredibly angry. And while it doesn't seem like I've said anything particularly nasty - it must just be the way I say things - but yeah, now I've made my Mum cry.

Dad looks at me as if to say: I hope you're feeling very pleased with yourself. 'Listen, this isn't getting us anywhere,' he says. 'Why don't you sit down and we can talk without having a slanging match.'

I'm not sitting down. I'm not sitting down because he's just told me to sit down.

'Nothing *is* goin on in my life! I live a very *boring* life!'

'Is that so?' He looks at me like he's already made his mind up. 'All we want is a bit of honesty.'

I'm making my Mum cry, I've made my Dad angry. What would happen if I was honest with them? Give me a break, Dad.

'I'll see you later.'

I won't have any choice; whatever time I come in, my Mum'll be awake with something to say. Yeah, remind me how old I am again.

Out in the jeep Sheena's still ribbing me about my

strange new look. Her and Axel are still in a laughter frenzy from watching this stupid show where people pretend to be doctors and tell people to take their clothes off, or tell people they're making a tv show and ask them to take their clothes off. I don't really understand the appeal. Sheena is starting to think that I'm part of some game, she wants to know why I didn't go the whole hog and wear a tie.

'How about a dickie-bow?' I ask. 'You like dickie-bows, don't you?' I have no idea why that might be hurtful, but it seems I can just about reduce anyone to tears at the moment. I wasn't even trying to be particularly nasty; the problem is Sheena's a bit of a soft touch right now.

We drive in silence as far as The Parsimonious Squirrel. Axel parks up, wishes me luck, says, 'I gotta get me some gas but I be back in fifteen. You not outside waitin, I come in for you, 'kay?'

''Kay.' He's so caring, he'd make such a nice boyfriend... for someone else. Him and Theo would make a lovely couple.

I climb out of the back of the jeep and grab Paddington, making sure he's still nicely taped up and not leaking any valuable bits of paper. Sheena tells me to take care of myself, see me in a minute etc, but doesn't mention the big-hatted duffel-coat-wearing bear I'm holding. It just goes to show how much people notice, especially when they've got other things on their minds, or when they really don't give a shit about you.

Axel booms off in his ridiculously aggressive accelerating way.

Note to self: if he shags like he drives... over

quickly, or most exciting ride of your life? *Discuss.*

So here I am standing outside The Acquiescent Squirrel on a windy summer's eve at quarter past eight. The clever idea I've got is that if I go inside now and try and find Harry, arrange to leave Paddington with him, he can sort it all out with Charlie Strange for me later. I'll explain a few things to Harry but not admit anything concrete. Assume he knows what's going on. Tell him to get his friend to check the bear's belly. Then say I want my babies back by twelve midnight or there'll be trouble. But it's the threatening thing I'm not so sure about. I was going to not take Paddington at all, arrange for a formal hand-over: here are the finsters, still doing well; okay, well, here's the bear with his arse full of notes. Now we're equal, let's forget everything. Instead I decided to just get it all over with.

So why do I feel like I want to just stay outside here till my good friends Axel and Sheena return, then drive off in the jeep with a happy dopamine grin on my face. Yes, everything went swimmingly, let's get out of here. If it wasn't for the finsters I'd be tempted to take that *head-sand-bury* easy way out. Instead I'm walking through the door of the pub, already blushing, waiting to get stared at. In my stupid big suit looking like a refugee from weight-watchers.

I don't want to just look like a complete fuckin idiot, standing here waiting, so the obvious thing I can do is look like a complete and utter fuckin idiot with a reason to be here. An alcoholic fuckin idiot.

The bottle-blonde barmaid smiles at me shyly - in a way that could be perceived as anything from general friendliness to mocking condescension - depending on your level of mental health.

'Hi, what can I get you?'

'I'll have a ... drink, please.'

'What would you like?'

'Beer, please.'

'Lager?'

'Please.'

'This one?'

'Thanks.'

'Pint?'

'Half.'

See, talking to people, it's really not that hard. I didn't want lager, I didn't really even want a drink, but it's so much easier to take the easy option.

'Take one for yourself.' There I go with that generosity thing again. I'm a changed person. Giving, giving, giving. Here, here's four thousand pounds - give or take the odd fifty quid. Have it. I really and truly don't want it.

I take a look around. There's a band crammed onto the tiny stage in the corner but not many people here to listen. In fact, there's five in the band: bass, keyboard, guitar-playing singer, glockenspiel and backing singer; then there's me, the barmaid and about five old men dotted around the pub staring into space. An attempt has clearly been made to make this a happening place; it is an attempt that has most certainly failed. So when I walk in here with my youth, my beauty, my suit - that stopped making sense almost as soon as I put it on - and my greased-back dark-red ponytail, flopping like a little pony's tail, it's no surprise that all eyes are on me. Or it felt like all eyes were on me. The reality is - as I take a good confident look around - no one could care less. Like anywhere else, a newcomer falls into one of four categories: fuckable, ignorable, fightable, laughable. I'm fitting into category two, which is better than I could have expected. Though when a man in a kilt is slurring the words to the *Wild Rover* at jet-engine decibels, no one's gonna pay you much mind.

'I've never seen you in here before,' says the barmaid, fighting against the backdraft of an amplified glockenspiel solo. 'Have you come to see the band?' She's wide-faced and lovely this thirty-whatnot barmaid, like a koala bear in a blonde wig. If she had an infant strapped to her neck you wouldn't be surprised.

'Meeting some people. One or other person, depending,' I say, floundering like a fish. 'Only popped in for fifteen minutes.'

'You goin somewhere else after?'

It's the youth and beauty not just the boredom, that's why she's talking to me.

'A club called Mattress,' I say, feeling strangely hip and trendy for once. Normally I'd have to say, no, I'm going home to count my freckles, y'know, it's boring but it's gotta be done. For once I have something exciting to say, 'Someone's birthday,' apparently.

'Sounds good. I've heard of that place. Heard quite a lot about it. Is that what Paddington's for? Birthday present?'

'No, no, well sort of.' Laugh, no viable explanation, just don't answer. 'Handing it over to one of the people I'm hoping to meet here. They... collect soft toys for this orphaned children's home they do charity work for. Don't know if you know one of the guys I'm looking for? His name's Harry. The other one's Charlie? Though I'm not sure if that's his real name.' She shakes her head like no bells are ringing. 'You must have seen Harry: head like a balloon with features and spectacles attached. Irish.' I've lost her now, lost her completely because one of the sad sack old men has managed to grumble his way to the bar and order another pint of stout. But I could always come back another day, when we're both feeling lonely, chat to her some more. And that's when I notice that one of the five space-staring old fellas is really vibrant forty-two-years-young-bachelor Harry the Boss. My desperate plan was soundly reasoned. Harry is in here; Harry is always in here. It's still only twenty-two past, so if I'm quick I can drop off the bear and get out of here before Charlie Strange even arrives. I have no desire to see him ever again.

'Harry!'

'Sunshine!'

Harry's laughing face, my serious complexion. I sit down next to him.

'Harry, I'll be as brief as I can. I've got people waiting for me outside.'

'It's nice to see you, Sunshine. Most unexpected ha ha ha,' laughter laughter laughter. My life is just a parade of laughing faces. It's like I've enrolled in clown school. I laugh back at him for want of anything better to do or say.

'Truth is, Harry,' he gulps at his drink, I maniacally tear up a beermat, 'I want to wipe the slate clean. I don't know how much you know about this.' I put Paddington on the table, trying to get him to stand up in his little rubber Wellington boots, but failing and sitting him back down on my knee. 'I've brought this for a friend of yours. I think you'll find it's all here.'

'I think you're losing me at this point.' Harry's playing dumb, or Harry is dumb, or I'm not explaining myself very well.

'I'm not really explaining myself very well. Harry, the point is, could you pass this on to him. This bear. To your friend.'

'You want me to give this teddy bear to my friend?' Harry's starting to understand the basics even if the gist is passing him by.

'It's all in there,' I say, patting Paddington on the head for the last time, and lying him on the table - face down in a puddle of beer - it's time he got used to his new lifestyle. I stand up and have a last quick sip of my lager and look at my watch: almost half past. I'm hoping Charlie Strange won't be early. I don't want to see him; I can't bear the idea.

'Tell him, your friend, about the fish...'

'Sit down, Sunshine, will you. Can you not start again from the beginning? I have to say you've lost me completely. What with your teddy bear and your fish.'

'He'll know what I'm talking about. You probably know what I'm talkin about.'

'Can I assure you that I don't,' Harry says, louder than is necessary now the band are taking a well deserved and much appreciated time out.

'I want the fish back tonight. If they're not back by the morning I'm going to the police. The *po*lice.' I start walking off. I don't even want to talk about this. I'm trying to be brave and strong and it's not a role I can keep up for any length of time. Harry comes after me.

'Sunshine, I've an idea what you might be talkin about, but only an idea. If yeh can explain ta me what's goin on, I can possibly help you, I really can.'

I shake my head, I don't want to cry, it isn't brave and strong and grown-up. I leave him standing at the door, Paddington tucked under his arm, getting fostered by Harry till his new daddy arrives to abuse and rip his valuable guts out for him.

Axel's back and ready in the jeep as scheduled. I jump in and everything's going to plan. Now all I need to do is wait and hope that for the sake of honour and Baby Kurt Kobain everything will be okay. As we speed off at neck-throttling speed I notice someone appear out of the shadows dressed from head-to-toe in white. I don't get a chance to check what shoes he's wearing. I'm on my way to have fun. I've got a lovely young woman to entrance with my wit, beauty and sense of the ridiculous. And I really need to have a serious talk with Axel about what the hell he thinks I'm playing at.

Fourteen

Do I have to repeat myself again? I'm getting fed up saying the same thing again and again. This is what I've got to tell him. How it feels like I'm playing the fool for them. No matter what he says, that's what it feels like.

We're parked outside *Mattress* but I'm not getting out of the jeep. I'm as grumpy as an owl in the Swedish summertime. I'm plain not happy. I want to go home and wait for my fish to arrive. But I need to be distracted by activity and alcohol while I wait, hope, dream, and try not to think that I may have done the most stupid thing ever. Four thousand pounds for four *fish*? Does Charlie Strange even have my babies? Did Harry actually have a clue what I was going on about? Will he etc etc etc. It doesn't bear thinking about, does it, Paddington? Paddington? Where are you when I need you? I'm all alone in the world. It looks like I'm going to have to get myself a sock puppet to talk to. Or a friend.

'Why am I here? I ask Axel again. 'I don't mean in general, on this earth, but here. Right now, right here, dressed up like a dog's breakfast, here? Hmm? And this is your last chance, favours or no favours, because I'm thinkin I might just go and get the bus home.'

I'm not wasting any more money on taxis.

'Hey, hey.'

'Don't *hey* me, Axel. Don't tell me to be fuckin *cool*. I am not cool, I don't want to be cool, I never will be *cool* –'

'There's no need ta be all –' Sheena butts her

blonde goat's head into the conversation, gives me a look that could sink a thousand ships. 'Let's try an be _'

'Okay, go,' I slump back against the leather seat, resigned to defeat after just fifty seconds of protest, 'Use me, abuse me, just tell me what the hell's goin on, *please?*'

'Listen, Sib, everythin *is* gonna be cool, 'kay? Here,' Axel unhooks his mobile phone from his shorts and presses it into my hand, holding it there as he tells me, 'any probs give Thee a call. Hey an if it rings? It be me or your bro wantin ta know what's happenin, 'kay? So answer it, we're here to help you, Sib.'

I have to ask, I have to try and ask without swearing, blinding or shouting, 'To *help* me do *what?*'

'This *thing.*' Axel and his grin, with his sunglasses on the top of his head at nine o'clock at night; in his shorts and vest like it's his first day in the country and he's not used to the whole going-cold-at-night phenomenon.

'This *thing?*' I repeat. He's not gonna tell me anything.

'One word,' he says.

'One word? I can think of two, the second one's *off,* the first you can pick from a selection of your choice.'

Axel says nothing. Sheena, Sheena for once has nothing to add or butt in, no wisecracks or jolly-ups, no put-downs or whinging complaints. Nothing. Sitting up front next to Axel in another seven year-old's tiger print t-shirt and arse-tight white pants. She's looking good, even I have to admit; all this recent trauma has added a sorrowful cast to her eyes. Before she was bright and open and bubbly and shallow, now she's got depths, or at least reasonably deep shallows. Or maybe it just goes to show the tricks you can achieve with a bit of charcoal grey eyeshadow and some thickly-applied mascara.

'Fact is,' I say, finally starting to climb out of this stupid doorless vehicle, holding onto the roll bar as I swing myself down. 'This Ava. This girl, woman, lady - that's *so wonder*ful she makes our Theo want to chuck his guts up – she's not, I repeat *not* gonna be interested in me.'

'Sib, you could charm the pants off anyone,' Axel grins like the flattering pig that he is. 'Hey, an if ya can? Theo say he want ya ta try an get her to go home with you, but y'know, see how it goes.'

'Err... wait, hello and *excuse* me? Chat her up was the first thing. Well, okay, given the *favour* I have to pay off, I agreed to that cos I reckoned that'd take about five seconds. Hello, how are you, what's your name, d'you fancy a drink, goodbye, good riddance, fuck off. But *take her home?* I *think* you've got some ridiculously inflated ideas about my girl grabbing prowess here.'

'Y'know what Thee say?'

I sigh. I don't know why I'm putting off the inevitable. Why don't I just go in there: I say hello, she says goodbye, as Sheena is my proof, that's my favour paid off. Spend the rest of the evening having Multiple Orgasms and drinking myself to oblivion before going home to find a washing-up bowl full of finsters on my front doorstep. Let the bells ring out and the people rejoice, our swimmers have been returned!

I ask him, 'What does Theo say?'

'Be tellin me it won't be the first time. Say that you an Equal Opportunities Employer - when it comes to your relationships. Don't matter what colour, creed, age or gender, you interested in em all.'

'Y'know, I'm having a strange feeling here. I'm feeling you've told me this once before but in very different circumstances. And whilst it was *almost* amusing then, as you can see, I'm not laughing any more, *Axel*. So I'll go for anyone, will I? Hey, you better watch out, Jeep Boy. Goin by that reasoning even you might stand a chance. But no, see I might not be bothered about what colour they are but I have to *like* em in the first place. They have to be exciting, interesting, intelligent, *sensual* people and all that bollocks people go on about. And that you're probably not interested in. I'm not gonna get off with someone just because they've got blonde hair.'

Though if they've got weirdly entrancing eyes I might give em a go.

'I think,' Sheena pipes up, 'what our friend here's tryin te say in his daft roondabout way is... well, Theo has this plan – I don't know what that plan is, so don't start lookin at me – and you're part of it. Yeh try yeh best an if she tells yeh ta *bog off*, then that's the way it goes.'

I'm resigned, resigned from my post of whinging killjoy, 'Let's get in there and enjoy ourselves.' I fake a smile, there's only one more thing for me to say, 'Axel? When this thing is done? No more favours, okay? Everything has been forgotten and nothing ever happened to you-know-what.'

'On my honour,' he pats his left pec in a meaningful military way.

'What's all this then?' asks Sheena, brightening suddenly. 'Secret yeh not tellin me?'

'Yeah, me an Axel are havin an affair.'

That makes her laugh, makes her laugh so much she almost trips over as she gets out of the jeep. Axel starts the engine.

'D'you want me to get you a drink while you're parking?' I ask him, still feeling generous, generous, generous.

He looks at me, crunching his eyebrows,

'Only you and Sheena stayin, all I doin is the drivin. Here,' he reaches across to the glove compartment, 'Theo found this for ya. Don't know if it'll be a whole lot of help.' He hands me a couple of sheets of folded paper. He grins and winks, then guns the jeep, off rampaging through the streets as fast as he can like some pixellated adventurer in one of those sad but addictive video games him and baby brother are always playing.

So this is *Mattress*, the famous Mattress that I've heard so little about. Comfy chairs and polished floors; hidden lighting and a mass of tight t-shirts, lipstick, cocktails and relaxed smiles. It looks like the kind of place where anything goes. Or our kind of anything goes quite acceptably.

I hold up Axel's pieces of paper and try and read them in the gloomy half-light. They're pages printed off the Internet, 'Top Twenty Best Chat-up Lines.'

Oh, brother. This is a fantastic help,

'My uncle's died and left me three million dollars on the stipulation that I find a life partner by Friday. Would you like a drink?'

Or would you prefer to commit suicide? I can offer you a variety of methods, Theo, though crucifixion would be my first choice. And if you have any trouble with that final nail, just give me a call.

'Are these cucumbers supposed to be soft? I guess I don't know much about shopping.'

That one might work I suppose, so long as you weren't actually in a greengrocers,

'Pardon me, but I have evidence that we were lovers in a previous life etc etc etc *Cleo!*'

I crumple the paper and flick it, Sheena comes back with our toxic orange cocktails; I don't ask.

'I bet you think me doing this is *very* funny.'

'I think it's quite exciting actually. I think you're very daring. I think I'll probably wet myself when you actually go up and talk to her.'

'Well perhaps you should go to the little girls' room now because things are just about to get exciting.' Ava has arrived. At least if my cursory look at baby brother's tear-stained photo is anything to go by. That's her walking in now: short black dress, black military-style boots, not unattractive slightly-broken Roman nose. I ask Sheena, Sheena confirms.

Axel's mobile starts beeping a Morse code message. I pull it out of my pocket and answer it; not surprisingly it's my little baby brother.

'Hey, how's it going? You spoke to her yet?'

'Give me a chance, she's only just got here.'

'I know, I know, I saw her. Well... good luck.'

'Yeah, thanks.'

Which as pointless conversations go, is pretty pointless. But then that's what mobile phones are for. Sheena asks me who it was but I just shake my head and don't even bother telling her because it'd take me more words to explain than Theo actually just said to me. I nudge her and point to brother's once and true love. 'So what d'you think of her?'

Ava standing in the doorway with her blonde friend like they're wondering what to do, whether to stay, whether to go.

'Hmm,' Sheena considers, 'she's not what you'd call picture perfect, is she, but she's definitely got something.'

'Would you shag her?'

'*What?* What d'yeh mean by that?' Sheena's face is a picture. It's a US Marine getting shot in the back with the words *WHY?* printed underneath. She doesn't understand. At all.

'But would you shag her?' Ava, chestnut brown hair, slim to the point of needing to be forcibly drip-fed; legs, arms, neck, ears, skin, all the usual elements that go to make up a healthy handsome person. Eyes that are too far away for me to do a colour check; busy chatting with her blonde-in-a-white-dress friend. Having a big discussion about whether to make an effort and stay or run straight back out and go somewhere more... more... *them*. They're not committed, hovering round the doorway, making their minds up.

'If I were a fella?' Sheena asks.

I shake my head, 'If you were you. If you were gonna shag anyone, would you shag her?'

'I'm sure she's a nice person,' says Sheena,

blushing and smiling, avoiding the crux and thrust of the question. 'She's not really my type, is she, to say the least, if yeh know what I mean?'

'Out of her and the blonde one, which one would you shag?'

'Which one do I think is the most *attractive?*'

'Which one would you shag?'

'Out of the two of them. It'd have ta be the blondie one.'

'You'd shag the blonde one?'

'Yeah.'

'Thanks, that's all I wanted to know.' I don't have any time to waste. It seems Ava doesn't like it in here. Her blonde friend, seems to want to stay, but she is of no interest. She's the one Sheena fancies and I wouldn't want to step on her toes.

Sometimes you just have to start doing something, one step then the next, till you're up to your neck and you have no idea how you got there in the first place. You have no idea what you're going to do or say next...

I walk till I'm close enough to headbutt her. I can either grab her and kiss her, punch her in the face, or say something.

'Hi! How you doin?' I say with a sudden burst of talking-to-strangers confidence I'm pretending to have. If my Mum can make herself do it, I can do it. It's learnt genetics. I'm like a pig that's been brought up by sheepdogs, it's not in my nature, but I'll give it a go.

Ava doesn't seem to have heard me. Or she's ignoring me. But this Ava, she does have eyes of the utmost quality. Dark brown and haunted, like a sheep

169

being worried by wolves. You might not want to shag her, but you do want to protect her. Now she's looking at me, wondering what I'm doing staring at her like a zombie.

'Would you like me to help you find somewhere to sit?' I don't know why I'm saying this. But I don't know what else I'm meant to say. Other than: do you fancy a dance? Or: my brother fancies you.

'I don't think there are any seats, are there? It looks a bit bizzy,' says Ava. Ava from Birmingham as she is henceforth known. 'We only come in to have a quick loook.'

'I'm sure we can find somewhere if we look hard enough.'

I seem to be under the impression that I work here. I've decided that's what I want Ava to think. Perhaps I lack confidence but unless she thinks I work here – unless I tell her I'm a plain clothes police officer and I'm about to arrest her – unless I'm a quiz show host about to present her with a random amount of money – why else is she going to want to talk to me?

I hold out my hand to show her the way then start to lead her into the crowded bar. It seems like the thing to do. They follow me, but you see, at this stage, my Mum, she'd be thinking at least one step ahead. She'd know what she was going to do next. I turn round to make sure they're still with me and end up banging into a table. I really should say *something*.

'Hi, how you doing?' The people at the table look up at me but they're not really sure why I'm talking to them so they don't bother replying. 'It looks like you're almost finished. Is there any chance we could sit down?'

'No,' says the one with the shaven head and thick arms.

'What about these two stools? No one's sitting here.'

'We're waiting for someone.'

'It's or-right, I don't mind standin,' says Ava in a voice that I am still trying to pretend is subtle, alluring and sophisticated. And it's not the Birmingham bit that grates; some of my best friends are from Birmingham, or would be if they'd been born there. It's that she sounds so hopelessly defeated. If a Jelly Baby could talk, it'd sound like Ava, 'I know you're gonna bite me head off. There's no point in complainin. It's me destiny.' All Jelly Babies come from Birmingham and they all sound like Ava. They just do and I'll say no more about it.

'Why don't you just push off,' the posh drunk with the moustache says.

So I sit down on one of the stools. It's as simple as that. Authority issues. Childhood trauma and incidents with bossy big kids. I'm just a big fat pain in the arse. Tell me not to do it and I'll do it.

I'm sitting down with a mental institute smile on my face and everyone's looking at me. Everyone in the world. I tap on the stool next to me and motion for Ava to come and sit. I'm so stupidly nervous right now that it would be better for all concerned if I was wearing a nappy. Ava looks at me with a vaguely horrified look on her face.

'We told you someone was sitting there,' says Thick Arms, standing up and trying to look menacing. But when you've just stolen close to four thousand pounds off the most dangerous man in the city, some thick armed idiot with a shaven head isn't gonna scare you much. I wave again for Ava to come over and sit, but she just keeps looking at me like you would some grizzly car accident: she can't take her eyes off me but she probably wishes she'd never seen me in the first place.

She's close enough so I grab her gently by the arm and pull her down next to me. I don't know what I'm trying to achieve but then that's pretty much the story of my life.

'We don't want to cause anny trouble,' says Ava sweetly, sitting on the stool and looking across at me with grateful but worried eyes, like she's wondering if I really am her lupine-face granny, or if I'm a wolf in a large bonnet and nightgown.

'No trouble *at all.* Now how about a drink? The cocktail I was drinking was very nice. Tastes like cream soda but makes you feel like someone's injected vodka into your eyeballs.'

And I've only had one. On an empty stomach. There has to be some explanation for the way I'm behaving. Other than fear, confusion and stupidity.

'I'm not really in the mood fer drinkin.'

'Go on. You may as well now you're here,' I stand up and sway slightly. Am I as scary to others as I am to myself?

'Err, go on then, I'll have a diet coke then please.'

'Yeah, vodka and coke,' says the blonde one even though I didn't ask her. I tell them I won't be a minute and push my way through to the bar. I need another toxic orange cocktail.

So I'm on my way back from the bar with a couple of triple vodkas and coke, and a toxic orange cocktail to add to the one I've just necked while I was waiting for the barmaid to give me my change. It was freezing cold but hot with alcohol and impossible to drink so quickly. I got one for Sheena but then I realised I don't know where she is. Still, it's not like I have to worry about Sheena, she could get Trappist monks talking. However, what *is* slightly worrying is that there's a bit of a to-do over at our table. Seems the people they were waiting for have arrived and claimed their stools back off us. Posh Moustache and Thick Arms staring over at me waiting to see what I'll do. Ava and her friend standing nearby – I'm frankly surprised that they haven't just run away like frightened Jelly Babies. I suppose I should run away as well that's just not my style tonight. Tonight I'm the Toxic Orange Avenger.

I go over and plonk my nest of drinks down on the table, pushing aside some empty crisp packets and cocktail glasses to make room. I'm doing that invading-personal-space thing again. The two newcomers look up at me. I don't say anything. Thick Arms stands up, Posh Moustache stands up and comes round and ever so gently grabs me by the arm.

'What do you think you're doing?' I ask as politely as I can. Looking at the hand on my arm like you would a strange insect. Feeling disturbed but scientifically curious: fingers as hairy as a ginger gibbon.

'Is there something goin on over here?' says a familiar shouty voice. It's not often I'm happy to hear that Geordie whine but I can't help smiling as angry-faced Sheena appears to my left and Posh Moustache lets go of me. 'Is everythin alright?' she asks me and I am feeling pretty shaken up, even if it is all my fault.

I start to tell her, 'We were sitting on those stools and then...' I look round but Ava and the blonde one have gone. I've lost the whole point of whatever it was I was trying to do. 'Ha ha ha,' I say. 'Got you! Got you got you got you!'

'Sorry?' says Posh Moustache.

'I was watching,' says Sheena. 'I think there's been a misunderstandin.'

'It was just a big joke,' I say like the drunken buffoon I am. 'I was only pretending, there's hidden cameras everywhere watching us.'

'What are you talking about?' Thick Arms wants to know.

'See, see,' I say, 'what I'm tryin to say,' blither blather tongue on strike, brain off on a two week holiday in southern Spain. 'We're, we're...'

'Ay, it was all a joke,' says Sheena. 'Yeh know that programme on the telly where the fellas play the tricks on people?'

They look at her with blank faces. I look at her with new found admiration and wonder. Sheena I love you. I don't really but for the purposes of the next five minutes in time I do. Save me, I'm drowning.

'No, what it is is we're both of us working up at the telly company, the BBC an that. The both of us. Thought we'd come out and play about a bit. Mess with people's heads you'd say, wouldn't yeh?'

She's talking to me now. I nod like a plastic dog in a car.

'A friend of ours is over there. With a camera and all of it. Hidden.'

'You're making a tv show?' For some weird tv related reason Thick Arms seems to have started to believe her. No one cares about me at all any more, that's the main thing. I'm free to drink my toxic orange cocktail. Make a start on the vodka and cokes. Wonder what I've done with Ava and the blonde one. I can't remember where I left them.

Sheena says, 'Nah, no so much makin. This is a what d'yeh call it – prototype.'

'Pilot,' says Posh Moustache. Posh Moustache is frowning like a maths teacher hearing the one about the poodle and the homework. Not convinced.

Thick Arms is grinning, 'This is so weird.'

But then Sheena works in public relations for a nuclear processing plant, if she can convince people two-headed fish are a good idea she can convince them of anything. She says, 'Aye, that's the one.' She grins her beautiful grin. The other people at the table are watching but if they're thinking anything I haven't got the brain cells to analyse what. 'Let me tell yeh,' Sheena touches one of those thick arms, but when she does it, no one could possibly complain. 'We tried this before. This is the first time we actually filmed it but you people were *so funny!* When you stood up and started saying what you said!'

'What did I say? Did I say something funny?'

Thick Arms, small brain.

'Is this a wind up?' Posh Moustache needs to get those frown lines tattooed on, save the effort of having to do all that forehead creasing.

'Of course it's a wind up,' says Thick Arms. 'That's the whole point, isn't it?'

'No, that's not what I meant.'

'Is this gonna be on tv then? What channel? I can't believe this.'

'I can't believe this.' Posh Moustache, no one's interested, no one's listening.

Sheena says, 'Aye well we'll have to work out all that when the time comes.' She looks at me. 'This one though? Absolute *what-a-star!*' She gives me a big lovely hug and whispers something in my ear. I can't hear what she's saying but I can see the look in her eyes and that's enough to tell me something.

Thick Brains wants to know more about when the show's going to be on and Posh Moaner wants to know more about why we think me sitting on a stool and arguing is funny and even if it is, what proof we've got that we're a tv production crew. Sheena smiles and smiles and touches as many arms as she can find to touch.

Meanwhile I need to slink off and find my Ava and that blonde one. I'm sure they're still here somewhere. They haven't even had a drink yet. They can't have left.

They have left. Fortunately it's started raining. Ava and the blonde one are standing in the doorway.

'Hi.' I'm not gonna bother with any of that clever making-conversation nonsense any more. 'How's things?'

'Not too bad,' says Ava. 'This bloody rain, ay?'

'Are you gonna go for a drink somewhere else?'

'Can't go anywhere at the moment... Do I know you?' she says. 'I'm sure I know you from somewhere. When you come up to me before, I was sure I knew you from somewhere. Otherwise I would've run a mile.'

'That's so funny because that's exactly what I was thinking about *you*. I thought I'm sure I know her. Ha!'

'Weird isn't it?'

We're both looking out at the rain. It's not pitter-patter, it's a tropical global warming style shocker. Nice to look at, but ridiculous to even think about stepping out in. We're getting speckled even standing here in the doorway.

'I *don't* know you, do I?' she asks again. The blonde one's having a fag, she probably hasn't even noticed I exist.

'Don't think so. Did you used to live in Birmingham?'

'Brought up there,' then she stops and smiles at what she's just said. I'm smiling back already. 'Why did you used to live there? No, I've seen you somewhere recently. I don't think we've spoken before though. I'd've remembered. Come back to me eventually.'

I nod, look at the rain; it's starting to ease off a bit, which is lucky or we'd all have to swim home. 'Sorry, I didn't catch your name?'

'I'm Ava and this is Felice.'

The blonde one nods and blows smoke at me. 'Hiya. Hey, never did get us that drink did yeh?' She's smiling when she says it like she's trying to be cheeky. Felice sounds more local. She sounds like a Liquorice Allsort. She just does and I don't want to talk about it.

I smile and mumble something and that's the full range of my conversational skills exhausted.

177

Though it does seem a bit odd that Ava's hanging around with the woman that shagged her boyfriend senseless, even if they are bessie mates, but that's not really a question I can ask. 'This weather,' I say looking out at it.

And that's when I see him. Across the road in the shadows watching. He makes my blood boil and my aura of confidence suddenly deflate like a paddling pool being bitten by a dog.

'We'd go home but we've got to have ourselves a *bit of a talk*,' says Ava. 'About certain things and certain people. Bit too noisy in there for us. Never mind anything else.'

'Oh yeah?' I turn round to look at her. She is very pretty. She's not perfect, we've accepted that, but she is very pretty pretty, very nicey nicey. 'Sounds a bit, y'know, sounds a bit like what my Mum and Dad say to me. *It's time we had a serious talk.*'

'I'd tell you but it's not the sort of thing you want to talk about to strangers. I'm not being funny but –'

'It's the sort of thing people talk about to strangers every bloody day,' Felice butts in. 'Did you not see the Ricki Lake show yesterday?'

'Ah but that's telly,' says Ava. 'I mean, not in real life.'

'I slept with her boyfriend,' says Felice like she should have it written in a caption under her name.

'It wasn't her fault though. It was his bloody fault. He got her drunk and told her I'd broken up with him.'

'He was cryin an everythin.'

'Thing is, what I was gonna be tryin ta say to her is I didn't really like him anyway. Always doing that running hot and cold thing. Flowers and champagne one minute then not calling me for days. Only thing is she still likes him.'

'Even though he is a bastard.'

'Can't believe I'm tellin you all this,' says Ava. 'Just once you start it's bloody hard to stop.'

We're all smiling and bonded and I'm trying to forget about who I've just seen on the other side of the road. The one thing I don't want now, as the rain starts to change from power-shower to dribble, is to be left alone out here.

'Doesn't look like the weather's gonna do us any favours. Let's go for a drink the three of us, shall we? You tell me your secrets, I'll tell you mine. Perhaps we'll remember where it is we've met before.' Was it when I was taking the bin out, or did you pass me on the way to the toilet at four in the morning? 'Here,' I take off my jacket and hold it over my head, 'we can all squidge in under this.' They crowd under and we start walking, 'And somehow you're still friends?'

'I think me and Felice'll always be friends.'

And that's when a car comes screeching to a halt by the side of us.

'What the hell's goin on?' shouts another familiar voice. Octavia winking her lights at us. Theo getting out and rushing towards us like a man on a mission, a look of fury in his eyes.

'What the bloody hell you doing here?' asks Jelly Baby Ava, suddenly ready to stand up for herself and protest. 'Are you bloody following me?'

Theo's not listening, 'What's goin on here? Do you want me to get rid of this... this *idiot* that's bothering you?'

'What idiot?' asks Felice. 'You're the only idiot I can see.'

Theo stops. If this was his plan. If this was what it was all about. What I was here for. If I was supposed to be so inept, embarrassing and annoying that he'd have to save them from me, then I'm sorry for being so *cool* and successful.

I don't say anything. Theo's face is a picture. It's a Mark Rothko painting that's almost completely black with just a whisper of mauve in the bottom right corner. It's meaningful but meaningless at the same time; it represents confusion and unhappiness.

Ava tells him, 'I've told yeh I don't ever want to see you ever again. Now bugger off, will yeh?'

Theo in his black suit, black tie, black shirt, in the rain. Sometimes wearing a suit isn't enough. I'm not even going to get angry with him for using me. I'm not even going to laugh in his face and rub his sorry face in the dirt. I'm not going to do that now, but obviously I'll hold it in store to do it at a later date.

'Come on,' says Felice, still protected from the elements under my big jacket with me and Ava.

We keep walking, Theo keeps staring, till we go round the corner and I am suddenly happy in my mindlessness. Then I remember something I should have remembered all along as I see who it is that's walking towards us from across the other side of the street.

Walking towards me with an insanely angry look in his poisonous green eyes. It's... guess who?

Fifteen

Who else could it be? Those big green eyes so violent and beautiful.

'Excuse us, but can I have a quick word with yourself,' he says in a voice that still sends electric shocks down my spine. I stop my smiling and get ready to buckle back into my continuing nightmare.

'Oh right, yeah, sure. Here,' I say to Ava and Felice, 'you can keep hold of my jacket, I'll meet you in there.'

'Where is it we're goin?' asks Ava like a hopeless Jelly Baby. Like she's just fallen down the side of the settee and she has no idea what's going on.

I move out of the dry safety of my suit jacket, towards Charlie Strange. Soon I'll be a drowned rat like he is; mad haired, mad eyed and generally mad. Standing in the gutter letting rainwater flood into his dirty white trainers. I tell my new friends, 'How about, errr ... that place over there? I've heard it's supposed to be quite good.'

'What?' says Felice, screwing up her face like she wants to fit it in her handbag. 'The Queen's Head? It's as rough as a builder's arse in there from what I've heard.'

I'm tempted to say the obvious; instead I tell them, 'Get yourselves out of the rain. I'll meet you in there in a minute.' They toddle off together beneath my jacket, one behind the other like a pantomime horse that's been stripped of its costume.

'Terrible weather, isn't it?' I say to Charlie Strange. 'Raining one minute, sunny the next.' Ha ha shut up.

He turns his back and walks away, then stops; he's expecting me to follow him back towards Mattress. I walk two paces behind, then stop as he disappears round the corner. There's a little Baby Kurt voice of anxiety in my head that's telling me to run like the wind while I've still got the chance. I listen to it for another second then Charlie Strange comes back.

'I thought you was comin with me?'

'Where are we goin? How did you know where I was?' The only person who knew, who he might have been able to ask, was that koala-faced barmaid. So that's pretty much who told him then.

We walk a few more steps then Charlie Strange stops and turns and grabs me by the front of my shirt, hurls me round till I'm pushed into a shop doorway. He holds me there, breathing heavily.

'I haven't got a gun with me today,' he says, spitting in my face, his eyes like a wolf. 'But I have got a razor, so don't fuckin *fuck* with me, okay?'

I nod as much as I can, as much as I can move, 'Okay.'

'*Okay?*'

'Okay.' Whatever you say, whatever you say, I'm scared so much I'm not sure I can breathe.

Genius, madness, love, hate, ecstasy and pain, I think I've just discovered they all look the same, it's only the situation that makes you think they're different. Right now Charlie Strange with his hellfire eyes, he is not in love with me, he probably doesn't even hate me, but I am convinced that he is insane.

'See, this is the story. I happen to be walkin down the street one day. *Today.* Then what happens next but a certain someone comes up to me spouting all sorts of foul and aggressive language. Tells me to meet em in a certain pub at a certain time. *Tonight.* Am I not correct in sayin that?'

'Yes... You're strangling me, please, could you -' I can feel tears forming, there's no money, there's no fish, there's just me now and I don't know what the problem is.

'So what I do —' he stops. The phone in my pocket is ringing. We listen to it ring its Morse code message, then it stops as suddenly as it started. Charlie Strange carries on, grips my collar a little tighter, 'I put on my best shirt and go down the pub, expecting to have a few drinks and a bit of friendly chitter-chat. But what happens? All there is is some God *awful* band, a few old lunatics and yours truly standing at the bar waiting, eating *three* fuckin packets of smokey bacon crisps and sipping at my lemonade. Y'see I don't drink alcohol, I don't know if you knew that about me, but I gave it up more than a few years ago. Completely. Just like that. Y'see alcohol makes me too aggressive.' He has a habit of spitting when he says his *esses*. 'Ended up I was waitin s'long I had my first pint for four years. See now I'm not happy in all sorts of ways.'

'I'm sorry, I'm sorry, I've tried to put everything back to normal. You can't have been waiting there too long, it's only after nine now.'

'I was waiting long enough, don't tell me how long I should wait.' He lets go of my shirt and steps back, which is a relief, then he says, 'How did you enjoy havin a gun pointed at your face by the way? What did that feel like?' He points his two fingers at me and *fires* them. 'Were you scared?'

'I'm so scared now I'm either going to wet myself

or have a heart attack.' I tell him the truth, he'll get nothing less from me from now on. 'I was petrified.'

'See I've only ever held a gun the one time. And I never got ta fire it. It didn't even have any real bullets in it, the truth to be told. For all I know it might have been a toy made out of plastic, though sure, it was heavy enough. So I feel I missed out there somehow. See I'd like to fire a gun. And right enough, the fella I lent it off, he's told me I can have a lend of it again, problem is, I need to pay for the first borrow of it. So I need money, d'ya understand?' I nod, there is nothing I don't understand, and there is nothing he could say that would make me disagree. 'But y'know,' he reaches into his inside jacket pocket, 'I've still got my knife.' It isn't a knife; it's a barber's cut-throat razor. He scratches it against the stubble on his cheek. 'So this is my question, and I'll be straight with you, you know that I know that you know who took the money. Agreed?'

Do I agree? That I know that he knows that I know that he knows who did it? 'Yes, yes but –'

'How can I put this more simply?' He looks up at the clouds, the rain, at God peering down through the murk. He takes a quick step towards me and pushes me against the shop door, the razor to my neck, '*Where's my fuckin money?*'

'I'm sorry, I gave it back, I'm sorry.'

He shuts up for a moment and looks round as a pair of laughing girls come walking down the road towards us. Charlie Strange looks at them then looks at me; he slides the razor into his pocket and holds my head in both hands like he's about to kiss me. Holds me so close, so hard, so *passionately*. The girls go past,

Charlie Strange steps back enough for me to breathe again.

'I want to be honest with you,' I say. 'It was an honest mistake and I thought about keeping the money, I really did. Then there was the break-in and you took all my friends' stuff and everyone was just so really scared and I couldn't help thinking that it was just all my fault. It wasn't worth it in the end, and that's the truth.'

'I don't know what you're talkin about. I didn't take anything of yours.'

'When you used my keys to break into our house? ... You took my fish?'

'Fish? Yeh keep goin on about *fish*. See I wasn't sure at first *who* had the money, and I asked a couple a people who are involved in all this, but it's not like you can believe people in a situation like this. People lie about money, it's only natural.'

'I've given it back, I promise you. I've given back the money. I gave it to Harry so he could pass it on to you. Tell him to look up Paddington Bear's backside, that's where the money is, that's where I shoved it all.'

He looks at me like he hasn't got a clue, like he doesn't believe a word. I feel like screaming for the laughing girls to come back, but what good would that do, other than get me four years in prison and perhaps slightly less of a stabbing.

'Y'know, the thing is, yeh tell me this and I truly want ta believe you, but I've not seen no money. All I've seen is a fuckin old sandwich and some fuckin – *I d'know* lipstuff an bollocks - which was no fuckin use to me. As far as I know, yous have still got it somewhere, hidden away safely. See cos yous seem to be doin alright for ya self. Goin out every night with these friends of yours, like you're *celebratin* every night.'

'No, no, please believe me. I mean –' what else can I say? 'I gave it back. I got to the pub early tonight and because I was in a rush and goin out with my friends – I handed it over to Harry. The money was hidden inside a Paddington Bear cuddly toy.'

'Ya best not be lyin ta me cos I know where ya live.'

'I know you do. You broke in.'

'How many *times* do I have to tell ya? I did *not* break and enter into your fuckin house.'

'So it was a coincidence that we got robbed the very next day after the other robbery?'

'I have no fuckin idea and less interest. I want my money, that's all I want.'

'I've told you, *I gave it to Harry.* I've told you, tell him to look up Paddington Bear's arse.'

'Wha? Now this is *Harry* your boss in the shop you're talkin about here? Not Harry the fuckin lollipop man that stands outside the school? I tell ya what I do know, I saw your man leavin the pub. This was just as I was gettin there. I was askin him where he was off to, he said he was goin ta visit his sick niece in tha hospital. Now since when he's had a fuckin niece I don't know... Fuck. *Fuck.* I'll fuckin kill him. Does he not realise how much money I owe to pay for the borrow of that shooter? I'll fuckin kill him I will.'

He pulls out the cut-throat razor again, and holds it up. 'Yeh better not be fuckin lyin or I will be back. Yeh can fuckin guarantee it. And don't you think yeh run away because I have ways of finding people. I know people that know people that can can find people.'

'Believe me, it's all there, it's all inside Paddington. Well, not the coins, I didn't think you'd be so worried about the coins.'

'How much coins have ya got?'

'About twenty-five quid left.'

'I'll be round ta collect em. Now listen, I'm havin ta trust yeh now by talkin ta yeh like this, and trustin people's not something I do if I can better help it. Y'see I messed up on this job and people are angry with me. It's not that they're not gonna pay me, it's much much worse than that. I'm gonna get hurt. So, if I have to hurt someone to get the money, if I have to hurt you, it's not gonna cause me too much pain. Though it will cause you a considerable fuckin amount if yeh lyin to me.'

I nod. I will do whatever I have to, whatever he wants, anything so long as he doesn't try and shave my ears off with that razor.

It's then that a car comes skidding to a halt by the side of us and I hear that familiar voice again.

'Hey! What the fuck's goin on?'

It's Octavia, it's Theo, suddenly putting a brave face on things, he must have been parked down the road since Ava had words with him. He must have been watching me here with Charlie Strange, wondering what was going on. He must have seen the cut-throat razor.

'Get in the car,' he says, looking at me with fear in his eyes, leaving the engine running but jumping out and coming towards us.

'Will yeh get in the car yeh self,' says Charlie

Strange. He folds away his razor and puts it in his pocket. 'A lift is just the thing I do need, that'll be very nice.' He walks round and opens the passenger door that Theo didn't have the sense to lock. He reaches inside and says something I can't hear to Theo. Theo getting back in to try and stop him.

Charlie Strange turns round to me, 'Here, here's your fuckin coat.' He throws my fox fur coat across the bonnet. 'It's not real y'know. It's not worth anything. I tried ta sell it. Couldn't find any fucker wanted to buy it. This wee motor though,' he caresses the sleek wet bonnet, 'there's a lotta people interested in purchasing this beauty.'

'Wait,' I say, grabbing my fake fur coat and pulling it on.

'What is it now?'

'About my fish. When you get the money off Harry. Bring them round and I'll give you your coins.' I'm wary of Theo knowing too much. 'Those coins I owe you. It doesn't matter what time of day or night, just come round as soon as you can.'

'Do I have to tell ya a-fuckin-gain? When ya talk about fish ta me the only thing that makes any sense is chips and batter.'

'But you kidnapped my fish,' I scream with the knowledge that I am the most pathetic human being alive. Nobody cares, nobody understands, nobody nobody blah blah misery.

'I'll kidnap your fuckin arse if you don't give over, now will you leave us. Your wee brother's kindly offered to give me a lift round to visit my friend Harry, but I'll see yeh the morrow no doubt. Now don't yeh worry, I'll not harm a single gelled hair on his head.

Provided he does everything I tell him and he puts some fuckin decent fuckin music on, instead of that Motorhead racket we had the last time,' Charlie Strange smiles and he gets in the car. My baby brother has the same startled, intense expression on his face that Charlie Strange had earlier. Except my brother isn't mad; he's fucking terrified.

Sixteen

I'm too confused and scared to know what to do or say or think. I've been standing here for I don't know how long but I'm suddenly snapped to attention when the Morse code bleeping phone in my pocket starts ringing again.

'Yeah?'

'Ho, how's it goin? How you doin?' It's Jeep Boy.

'He's kidnapped Theo.'

'*What?*'

'That guy, the guy, the man, the one outside our house today, earlier. The one I was telling you about. Charlie Strange or whatever his name is.' I'm crying and shouting and my words are spilling out too fast to make any sense to anyone.

'*Whoa.* Whoa there. D'ya wanna start from the beginning and tell me what the *fuck* is goin on?'

'He said he won't hurt him,' I can't even remember what he said. I remember the beautiful laughing dancing eyes, as happy as a lion before it eats a nice buffalo breakfast. 'He said he only wants a lift. He said he wants Theo to drop him off,' huh huh, heaving chest panic attack, 'at Harry the Boss's house.'

'So... I don't get it? Where's the problem?'

'He's got a bloody cut-throat razor in his pocket!'

'A razor with *blood* on it?'

'*No,* a bloody fuckin swearword one. A knife thing, y'know? That old people use for shaving purposes.'

'But it's in his pocket, right?'

'So?' What is wrong with him? Sometimes it just isn't right to be *cool* – not when your brother-stroke-best friend has just been bloody *kidnapped!*

'He can get it out of his pocket, y'know, the razor. He's got hands and fingers. Though Theo might not if Charlie Strange decides to cut them off for him!' The gang of lads heading towards me are suddenly silent as they go past this screaming loon in the soaking wet fake fox fur. I'm so disappointed it's fake, but then why else would they be selling it for £2.50 at Barnados. I want to be coated in animal skins, I want to be a cave dweller, I want to be alive before the invention of bloody fuckin swearword mobile phones.

'Listen, Sib, we gotta be –'

'Don't *bloody* say it. Don't say it, Axel, I swear I'll smash this phone into a billion pieces. I *can't* call the police. What *can* I do? How am I goin to get my fish back? You haven't got any answers so don't start tellin me what to do.'

'Yo, listen, okay? Hey, here's what I'm gonna do. Yeh any idea where they goin?' I tell him Harry's address. 'Right, that's just round tha corner from here, right? I get round there. I'm gonna give Thee a call while I'm travellin.'

I'm suddenly at a loss, confused that someone else is taking control and siphoning away my despair, 'You can't call him, can you? I've got your phone.'

'What?' he says. 'You think I only got the one phone? I got a stack of Nokias here, Sib.'

Which makes me remember him sweating in the cellar with his three phones on the go. I was distracted at the time, but now I have to ask, 'Why've you got more than one phone?'

I can hear him moving, jogging down the stairs, the front door absolutely slamming shut behind him.

'Need extra phones for my business deals,' he says.

'What business deals? You don't get dressed most days.'

'I works from home a lot of the time.' He squeaks his jeep's alarm off. 'What, you didn't know about that? Hey, yeh be tellin me ya believed all that bull about my Pop buying me tha house. Shit, Sib, I pays for everything I got.'

I don't want to sound like my Mum, but a sudden question does spring to mind. 'Axel, are you a drug dealer?'

'Aint gonna answer that one over the airwaves, Sib. I'm pleadin the Fourth Amendment.'

'Axel, it's the *Fifth* Amendment.' I've watched enough cops shows and chat shows to know that.

'Yeah? Well whatever, I'm rollin, I'll call ya soon.' And as Jeep Boy zoots off I'm starting to wonder if he's ever even been to Miami on his holidays. If he hasn't just spent his life listening to rap records and making up stories. A drug dealer? Him? The only thing he deals is a card when he's playing pontoon. But what do I know about anyone else's secret life? How much close attention do I pay to anything else but me and my babies?

I look at the phone with its list of saved numbers, as I thought, Sheena's in there, I call her as I walk towards The Queen's Head. She answers with a drunken squeal. 'Axel, how yeh doin?'

'It's me.'

'Ooh, hello *me*. How yeh doin? Wasn't that an *absolute* cracker just before with those people. I've never laughed so much for ages.'

'Yeah, I mean, no, everthing's rubbish, it's all

gone terrible. Theo's been kidnapped and my fish have been kidnapped. But that was yesterday – this afternoon – I'm all mixed up.'

'*What?* I don't understand! What's happenin?'

'Sheena, wait there, I've just got to go and speak to Ava and her friend and then we've got to go home.'

'Right, right, no problem. I'll order us up a taxi.'

She's sober and sensible suddenly, like someone who isn't on their fourth toxic orange cocktail. I put the stupid phone back in my pocket and rush across the road, and tear through the door of the pub, my eyes tracking round past the usual groups of hoary old geezers and withered specimens. Ava and Felice in the corner, as out of place as a pair of daffodils in a concrete factory.

'Hey, how's things?' I say, I want to be quick, I don't want to get into a screaming, heart-rending your-ex-boyfriend's-been-kidnapped scenario.

'Not so bad,' says Ava. 'Waitin on your arrival. Here's ya jacket, it was very kind of you to lend it.' She smiles a big genuine smile that makes you feel like you're the only one she's ever smiled at, that makes you feel maybe she is the one after all, that no one else will come close however hard you look.

'Err... sorry, forgotten what I was goin to say there.' I take the jacket. 'Thanks.' I'm flustered, I'm lost as to which lies I'm telling, which truths I'm hiding. 'Listen, I'm in a bit of a tangle, thing I've got to do, I'll tell you all about it some time.' As if I'm ever going to want to speak to them ever again. Though they are nice, I'm not saying they aren't. They're not my sort of people. 'Is it possible I could take your number and give you a call?'

Ava starts telling me her mobile number, but as there's no way I'll remember it - and I don't even want it and I don't know why I'm even asking for it - I ask her to write it down on the back of a beer mat and promise I'll be in touch, then leave them to have their big talk. Ava says, just as I'm going, 'Do you know Theo? Cos I'm thinkin that's how I might have met you before.'

'The guy with the car? I have met him before, yeah.'

'That'll be it then.' She smiles and I have to admire her and her face that's been designed by a Zen gardener on God's day off. Then I'm out of there and running like some soaking wet loon in a fake-fox fur coat. Round the corner, up the road and panting all the way to Mattress.

Sheena's waiting outside.

'Good news,' she says. 'I've just been on the phone te Axel. He says everythin is gonna be alright. He's there and he's handlin it. And he says he's got a surprise for yeh. Something he wants to show you.'

Yeah yeah puff pant puff pant, 'What's he handlin anyway? What?'

'He says, *everythin.*'

'Well that's alright then.' I lean against the bar's frosted glass front window and try and get my breath back. If there was a party on in there tonight, we never did find out whose it was. Our minicab's waiting already, 'I'll call him,' I say. 'Find out what's goin on.'

'Hi there,' says the driver as we both slide into the back, 'think you still owe me some money,' he says to me. It's Abdul's – Mr Halal Sandwich's – brother. He gave me a lift home a million years ago. Or yesterday afternoon, whichever was earlier.

'I paid your brother,' I tell him, finding Axel's number and dialling like I'm an experienced mobile user.

'Well he aint paid me, I'll tell you that. Where we goin, home, is it?'

Sheena tells him, puts her arm around me like she can sense my fear-terror-fear-terror. Why, just why the fuck don't I call the fuckin police and be done with it?

'I'll pay you now, don't worry about it,' I tell the driver. 'I'll pay you double. I'll give you whatever money you want.'

It must be the mad loon panic, but the really-quite-nice driver, turns his plonk-plonk disco music down and tells me it's cool. He says, 'Only like sayin, y'know what I mean? I know yous is gonna pay me. Just pullin your leg, innit?' Then he turns back like he's thinking bad thoughts about me, thoughts he is quite bloody entitled to think. Axel's not answering; I'm going to his voice mail. I try a different number from the list, Axel 3, this time he picks up.

'Ho, Sib, what's happenin?'

'What's happening with you?'

'Hey, we're cool. We're cool here. Thee's here, you want a word?' He passes the phone over to my little baby moonfaced brother.

'I've been hearing bad things about you,' says Theo. Knocking me sideways because that's the last thing I'm expecting to hear. I should be angry with him. I should feel used and soiled and boiling with rage, not glad to hear his gruff little voice. To think I used to look after him and help him cross the road and bully him when I was bored and ignore him when I wasn't. It's a sibling thing. It's understandable. And now here we all are. Here we all are... still alive.

'You're alright? You're alright?'

'No thanks to you! And my car – what's all this that's been goin on with the car?'

'What's Axel been sayin?'

'Never mind Axel, it's what your friend told me –'

'Did he say anything about my fish?'

Theo laughs and says something to Axel in the background. Life's such a parade of jokes and laughter, laughter and jokes with hardly any tears.

I'm waiting, I'm waiting. Then he comes back,

'Listen, about my car,' he starts.

'Sorry Thee, I think it must be a bad line –' crackle crackle '-I'm losing you.' I hang up. I don't have the patience for his whinging right now, but then I never have patience for his whining. I tell Sheena baby brother is fine and she gives me a lovely-lovely-no-longer-lonely hug. And I just can't help myself. I hug her back and this time I don't want to let go.

Seventeen

This time she doesn't want to let go. I rest my head on her shoulder and I'm tempted to take a bite out of her soap-smelling neck. Sheena's more of a Gingerbread Girl than a Jelly Baby but she certainly smells of sugar and spice and all things nice. It's no wonder I've always hated her.

'At least we can relax now,' she says. 'You fair had my heart goin there, y'know. I was goin crazy wantin ta know what was goin on. But Axel says it's all just been a big misunderstandin. Don't know what it's all about though. Have ta get yous to tell me sometime. What a night! And that thing with us doing the pretending about being makin the telly programme. *Sooo* funny!'

'Yeah.' My babies, my babies have gone. Perhaps they did go flying out the window; I just didn't have the heart to look. I was just too scared of what I might find. So the burglary was just common criminals. Common criminals with a key or else a *very sophisticated* way of getting in without making a mess. Not that they didn't mind making a mess once they got in. Me thinking it was Mr Armed Robber again. Or. Me believing Mr Armed Robber when he's turned around and denied having anything to do with it. But denied so damn convincingly. I'm just too upset and hopeless to think.

'I'll tell you all about it when we get home.'

Sheena nods and we sit in silence while the traffic lights change from red to green. Then she says, out of the complete-and-absolute-no-idea-what-she's-talking-about blue, she says, 'If there were only three people left alive on the earth, you, that Ava and her blondie friend –'

'Felice? She was quite nice actually.'

'So she's the one you'd pick? I mean, like you were asking me.'

'Which one I'd shag?'

Sheena nods. I'm not sure my brain's really up to this right now.

'Are there any other creatures left alive in the world? Any dolphins or dogs?'

'No, nothing.' She is slurred and blurry-eyed. Happy and drunk. I was dribbing and blurry about half an hour ago; it's amazing what a shot of adrenaline can do.

'No Koala bears anywhere or big Jelly Babies?' I don't know what I'm saying, Sheena certainly has no idea, she knits her dark eyebrows and moves away the arm that's been hugging round me.

'I feel so drunk,' she says and looks out of the window as we zip through the streets as fast as a taxi can go. 'Oh God! I've just remembered!' she turns back to me with a big grin on her face, 'I'm not sleepin in my room t'night. Because I've been bloody well robbed, haven't I?' She laughs as only a seriously drunk woman could. 'I'm sleepin with you,' and she hugs me again.

'That'll be nice.' I can't help but get carried away; I'm laughing with her as well as at her.

'*Won't it?* Now tell me, who would yeh rather spend the night with, me or Axel?'

We're arriving, Sheena wants to pay with her credit card but I tell her I'll take care of it, it's my last generous act before I return to a life of penury and penny-pinching meanness. I give Abdul's brother the money for the two taxi rides and tell him to keep the change, because really, I couldn't care less about money any more.

'Go on, who?' she says, as I lead the way up the path and open the front door, then do my usual rush to 3467 the alarm – which of course isn't on, because Mum and Dad are here to protect us.

'*Axel?* What makes you ask that?' I say as quietly as I can and wave for Sheena to follow me as I start trudging up the stairs to my room. I have no idea what time it is, but it feels like bedtime. Mum and Dad have probably gone to bed already, if they haven't, I'm not in the mood for another bloody fuckin swearword *chat*. And of course, there was no washing-up bowl on the doorstep. No happy swimming Satan, Judas or Lorraine. No long lost Baby Kurt Kobain. Gone forever to a ghost fish town in the sky where it's always raining flakes of food and there's pirate ships for every finster to swim through and hide in, even the smallest fry is well-fed and happy.

'Have you not seen the way he looks at you?' asks Sheena in a voice that's louder than I would like. Then she tells me to wait and goes clattering back down and into the kitchen, coming back with two mugs and a bottle of Polish vodka from the freezer. I wait for her outside Jeep Boy's room. The light's on, but that means nothing. He's probably out dealing crack-cocaine. Or dealing an ace and the jack of clubs to some pontoon addicts. Him a dealer? He couldn't sell meat to a butchers. Though I'm probably not the best one to talk about his powers of persuasion. Truly, I have no idea what Axel does with his spare time. And even less interest. But that isn't going to stop me from interrogating him and strip-searching him the next time I see him.

I open the door to my unusually tidy room with its double bed, wardrobe and chest-of-drawers arrangement, artsy postcards on the wall and the big old fish tank. Tankgirl still stuck to the glass like chewing gum on the bottom of a shoe. I drop my keys on the floor and collapse on the bed. Sheena pours me a vodka and puts the mug in my hand, then pulls off her trainers and sits down next to me on the bed, taking off her tiny ankle socks and pulling fluff from between her red-painted toes. She has a quick sip of her vodka and pours some more into my mug, then unzips her trousers, pulls them down and steps out of them.

'And the way you talk to him when you're havin a go? His face?' She turns round and leans over to look at me, uncomfortably close and trouserless. 'He's like a puppy that's been smacked. He still loves you but he doesn't know what to do.' She collapses back onto the bed next to me, curling up underneath my outstretched arm.

'*Axel?*' I laugh nervously. '*No.* He looks like that at everyone.'

'No he doesn't. And stop evading all the questions or I'll start callin ya *Sib* and we'll see how you like that.'

'You're sleeping here t'night, aren't you?'

'I most certainly am.'

'I was just reminding myself. What was the question again?' I sit up to give me some distance and get me some more vodka.

Sheena dropping her kecks and lying on my bed. Repeat that image and try to understand. It's probably just me but I always had the feeling that Sheena didn't even like me. We don't get on. We're like a pair of cats meeting at midnight in a back garden somewhere. We don't actually come to blows, but we spend hours whining at each other. It's probably about territory or dominance or jealousy. Or veiled sexual attraction. But that's what I don't like about psychology, it starts you thinking about things you'd rather just ignore.

Sheena's yawning, her eyes shut; she'll be asleep in about five minutes. 'I don't even remember there being a question,' I say with a tired ha ha ha.

'Who would yeh rather spend the night with, me or Axel?'

'Err... Whoever takes up less space in bed?'

'Well at least yeh didn't say whoever's not got the smelliest feet cos mine are *mingin* ta night.' She giggles to herself then goes silent and it seems like that's the end of her. I'll have to shift her round and get her tucked in before I climb in beside her. In the morning we'll just have to see what happens. A fresh start.

I go over to drag shut the curtains, but instead I decide I want to smell the air outside and try and crack open the window. It was open earlier during my flying fish shenanigans, then again when my Mum creaked it open to get some much needed fresh air, but I've slammed it shut again since then. So I have to give it a bit of a shove before it yawns back open again, and leaves my fingers with a nasty coat of chipped off paint and window fungus.

I stand there listening to the wind and looking at the stars. Somewhere out there are my babies, swimming in fish heaven, swimming in circles in a washing-up bowl. Somewhere out there is my real birth mother, my real spunk father, doing whatever they're doing, in heaven, in hell, in Lower Ancoats or Cleethorpes. In a different dimension, in the future, in the past, there's me wrapped in a tea-towel in a bus shelter age eight hours; there's me wrapped in a blanket in a bus depot aged eighty. Back where I started except now I've upgraded from summer tea towel to winter blanket.

I look at Sheena on the bed, her blank face that could be thinking anything, but whose mind after too many toxic orange cocktails and vodka is probably as blank as her face. I leave the curtains open so I can lie in bed and look at the moon. It's gonna be hot again tonight. I grab an x-large t-shirt from a drawer and go down to the bathroom as quietly as I can to brush my teeth and get washed and changed. Sheena's too drunk to be bothered with washing or brushing so I'll leave her where she is.

I go back to my room trying to be as quiet as I can, switch the main light off and slip into bed. All I can think is, in the morning. In the morning everything will be better. In the morning everything will be different. In the morning everything will be worse. In the morning is when all hell will break loose. Harry, Detectives Harper and Call-me-Jill, Satan, Judas, Charlie Strange, Lorraine, Axel, Mum, Dad, Theo and Baby Kurt Kobain. I've still got the coins, I've still got too much knowledge to be safe. If I don't get my fish back I want half of the money. I'll demand it. If I don't get my babies back I'm going straight to the police. I'll leave the country, I'll dye my hair purple, I'll get a tattoo, I'll do what I have to do, they won't get away with this. They. Harry, Charlie Strange, *whoever*, I don't care.

'Come on then,' says Sheena, not quite as asleep as I thought, 'get in and give me a cuddle.' She starts laughing and I start laughing and trying to shush her, we're both just overcome by the drunken ridiculousness of it all. And I'm not even very drunk any more. 'If there was just me and you left on earth alive,' says Sheena. 'Let's pretend. Everyone else has been and gone and died. Would you then?' Her eyes twinkling with little pieces of stardust.

There are invitations, and there are invitations. There's the open back door that the burglar can't resist. There's the written card you're expected to r.s.v.p. before a wedding. And there's the desperate person asking if you'd shag them if they were the last person on earth.

I kiss her and she kisses me. We kiss. We kiss kiss kiss kiss and kiss more. No drugs tonight. The odd toxic orange cocktail and a slug or three of freezing Polish vodka. Brain a bit frozen but sense enough to know what's happening and sense enough to enjoy it. Taking off the size seven-year-old tiger t-shirt, taking off my x-large t-shirt. Her tit tattoo, my nipple ring, surprise and rabid fervour, and the door slamming open and a familiar voice screaming out, 'What the fuck d'you think you're doing?'

203

Eighteen

'What the *fuck* do you think I'm doing?' I shout back at him as loud as I can without downright shouting my head off. 'What the fuck are *you* doin? Coming storming in here without a by your leave.' I don't know what a by-your-leave is, but apparently you normally need one. 'You've got no bloody right.'

'Haven't I now?' shouts Theo. 'Well I'm glad I did!'

'I bet you bloody are,' Sheena shouts back at him, huddling under the quilt next to me as shocked, angry and bloody plain *embarrassed*-back-to-reality as I am.

'Listen, forget all that,' says Theo. Then he goes silent while he thinks about what he's trying to say, 'Look, I'm sorry I barged in on you, but I didn't realise Sheena was...'

'Sheena's staying here tonight because Mum and Dad are in her room.'

'Yeah, I remember, I heard, I mean – but forget all that. About my car.' His bloody bloody *bloody* car. I wish I had smashed it into a tree or driven it off a bridge - just to get rid of the blasted thing. 'Your so-called *friend* -'

'Who? *Charlie Strange?*'

'I don't know what his name is! You know the one I mean.'

'Well I can tell you, he's not my friend!'

'Seems you lent him *my* car so he could drive *two hundred miles* to visit some friend of his! He even had the cheek to tell me – *I put petrol in* – like that's going me make me feel any better!'

I'm getting fed up with this, Sheena's keeping

out of it, she has no idea what's going on and the good sense to realise that this is nothing *whatsoever* to do with her. 'Theo, I didn't *lend* your precious car to anyone. Charlie Strange *stole* it.'

'Well why didn't you go to the police?' He's screeching loud enough to wake the neighbours, let alone Mum and Dad. I put my finger to my lips and point downstairs. 'I don't care who hears,' he says, but says it more quietly like he doesn't want to move into a parent-controlled environment at this time of night either. I have no idea what time of night it is. I suspect it's probably not very late, I certainly wasn't thinking much about sleeping when baby brother came barging in.

'Theo, I haven't really got the energy to discuss this with you right now.'

'Ha! I *bet* you haven't.' The stupid suit-wearing goon. Doesn't he realise his suit has no power against me. I'm the anti-suit. He's my little brother and as such I don't have to listen to him, humour him or do what he says, whatever he says.

'This isn't about your bloody beloved *car*, Theo, and you *know* it.'

'It's got *everything* to do with her -'

'With *her*, yes, with her, *Ava*. My new friend? And her bessie mate, Felice, who frankly, brother, if you play your cards right you might still stand a chance with.'

'Who? What?'

'*Felice*. She's the one that you should be going for. She's blonde, she's pretty, she's -' I'm tempted to say, *as rough as a builder's arse,* 'she's *nice*. You liked her, didn't you, Sheena? You thought she was attractive?'

'Yeah, she is, very pretty,' says Sheena, smiling. 'Though I only saw her from a distance,' she says, spoiling it somewhat.

'You reckon?' Theo had a speech in his head, a cranky old diatribe. I seem to have crashed his train of thought, 'but what about -'

'*Ava? She* won't mind. Go for it, brother, do it. Give her a call, give Felice a call. It's not too late, do it now.' I don't know what time it is, but Felice didn't look like the sort of girl that goes in for early nights and mugs of cocoa. 'There, my jacket. That stupid big jacket Axel got for me. There's a beermat in the pocket. Give her a ring. Tell her you're from a tv production company and you want to meet her for a drink.' Actually, as far as I can remember it was Ava that gave me her number. So it probably wouldn't be a very good idea for our Theo to call that number. But it would be amusing in a cruel and pointless way.

'*What?*'

'What? What are you talking about? Just do as you're told, can't you? Remember I'm the elder sibling here. I know best.'

Theo grins, like he's embarrassed to be taking orders; but he's going to do as he's told for once. He goes for the jacket, then stops. 'I've got her number anyway. I err... sent her a text message once.'

'Theo, for God's sakes, don't try and be coy about it, we all know you shagged her.'

'Yeah, sorry.' He smiles bashfully like the silly little boy he is.

'Now if you wouldn't mind?' I say turning my back to him and snuggling down under the covers with

Sheena. 'Oh, and switch the light off on your way out. I'm sure you can understand that I'd much rather discuss all this *car* business in the morning.'

He can't help laughing a little at me and Sheena and our heads and bare arms peeking out of the top of the duvet.

'See you in the morning then,' he says. 'And remember, I'm still not happy about this.'

'Give her a call. Make someone happy for a change.'

'You think? You reckon it's worth a try? I do like her you know.'

'Course you do, now switch off the bloody light.'

'Oh, I've just remembered. I've got something to tell you.'

'Tell me in the morning.'

'Axel's got a surprise for you.'

'I bet he has. Tell him I'll see him in the morning.'

'He says to tell you he's got something to show you that's going to put a smile on your face. Says for you to come downstairs.'

'Theo, in the morning for God's sake. I'm not getting out of bed now, I'm too tired.'

'Yeah, right, well whatever.'

He shuts the door with a bit more of a slam than is really necessary. Sheena still thinks that it's the funniest thing that's ever happened. Then she stops laughing when I touch her where a friend really shouldn't.

I'm not asleep but I'm in a gentle half-awake daze. Sheena's breathing softly, snuggled against me, our legs knotted together and twisted like a pigtail. It seems like I don't notice it at first or I try and pretend it's part of a dream, but there's someone knocking at the door. I try and ignore it and pretend to be asleep in the hope they'll go away. It's a gentle knock but it isn't stopping.

'*Sib*? Hey, Sib, it's me. Can I come in?' It's Jeep Boy and he's already sneaking in, letting in a shaft of light from out on the landing. 'Wondered if we could have a kind of a chat?'

'Don't turn on the light.' I say in a panicked whisper, pulling the duvet up higher so it's up to my neck and over Sheena's face.

''Kay, no problem. Sib, I was just thinkin, y'know?' He's standing holding the door handle but I can tell he wants to come over and sit on the bed. 'Feel like I needed ta see yeh. Don't know if Thee said anything to ya, but I kinda got something for ya. Then thought maybe we could have a little talk again, or y'know, somethin else?'

I try and sound as pissed off as I actually am, 'Axel, *I'm too tired.*'

'Oh, if ya... I don't wanna push it.'

'Axel, we're friggin too tired ta talk, now push off.'

'*Sheena?*'Axel's slightly more than surprised, he doesn't know what's going on, but it's okay, we've got the perfect excuse.

'My Mum and Dad are in her room.'

'Hey, yeah, forgot about that, cool.' Axel changes his tone completely. 'Right, I'll leave it till the morning then. Aint nothin that can't wait.' He can't get out of here fast enough. 'Night, Sheena. Night, Sib.'

He shuffles out, gently shutting the door behind

him, making me feel a bit sorry for him, left down there all on his own. It's a big bed, we could have gone tops and tails; he could have had his head down next to Sheena's smelly feet. It would have been better than being on his own, but then I've not had a whiff of her feet yet.

'What did I tell yeh?' says Sheena. 'He's like a horny dog sniffin round after yeh. You'll have ta watch out or he'll be pissin on your doorstep, leavin his scent to keep others out.'

'Sheena, you're a disgrace. If my Mum could hear your language, she'd think a lot less of you, I tell you.'

'You're a bad influence,' she says and we kiss and tie ourselves into more knots than a boy scout could ever dream of.

Then it seems that I'm opening my eyes but there's a moment of hesitation where I'm wondering if I'm in a dream or am I awake, before I realise, the nightmare has returned. A man in a black ski-mask is standing at the foot of the bed. I sit up and want to scream but I don't say a word. Except. Except this isn't our usual ski-masked invader. He's shorter and even in the dark I can see that he's wearing a white tracksuit and carrying a little sports bag over one shoulder. He puts his finger to his lips and points at Sheena, flat out, exhausted, drunk and asleep by my side. I cover her with the duvet and reach across to grab my x-large t-shirt from the floor.

The moonlight's shining in and my eyes are getting adjusted and that's when I see the gun he's pointing at me. He says, 'Don't try anything silly,' in his singsong Welsh voice. 'You don't want to make this any worse than it already is.' I pull on my t-shirt and have a look to see if I can see where I threw my pants.

'Who are you? What d'you want?' It's the middle of the night, I'm tired and it's dark, but even so, even considering how puddled and muddled my mind is, I've a fair idea I know the answer to both questions. He's pointing a gun at me. He wants the money. He's wearing a white tracksuit and speaking with a Welsh accent. It's Mr H Big Spender from yesterday, the Welsh Clint Eastwood. He comes closer.

'Now we don't want ta wake up your friend here, do we now?' He pulls back the duvet to look. 'Very nice.' He looks around, 'I see you've had some work done round the house since I was last here.'

'I'm sorry, I don't understand.'

'Had a bit of a tidy round. Fitted a new lock on the front door as well. That was a bit disappointing. Luckily I took the back door key with me so it wasn't so hard to get in. But I tell yeh, you wouldn't *believe* how angry I was last time I was up here mind.'

'What d'you want?'

I sort of know what he wants. He wants back the money he lost. I don't know who told him I had it. I don't know why he thinks I've still got it.

'I want my money, that's what I want,' his voice sing-songing the words like he's some happy-go-lucky chappy and not a homicidal killer pointing a gun at my face.

'I haven't got your money. I haven't got *anyone's* money.' I think I've been through this before. He brings the gun up close so it's touching my cheek, slides it across so its under my nose, pressing forward so

I'm forced to move my head back, then grazes it across till its resting against my left eye. The cold metal barrel black and enormous and all I can see. All I can think of.

He sniggers and takes a step back and it feels like I'm breathing again. He points the gun at the bed. 'If I shoot you, shoot you dead, you won't be able to tell me where the money is and that'll be a waste.'

Sheena says something in her sleep and starts scratching her itchy nose. Then she turns over so she's sleeping on her back, her mouth dropping open.

'However, I could shoot you in the leg. Or, this is even better. I could shoot your *friend* in the leg. Or the head. Then you'd tell me wouldn't you. If I shoot her in the knee and tell you I'm going to shoot her in the head, that's probably best. Then you'll want ta tell me everything. I'll be like your best friend. You won't keep any secrets from me.' He stops and looks at me from behind the black-ski mask. 'So tell me, give it to me, and we can all go back to bed and have a good night's sleep.'

'What's it – I don't understand – what has it got to do with you?'

'Give me my *fuckin* money or I start shootin.'

'Hmm, what time is it?' asks Sheena, reaching for me, starting to wake up.

'It's okay, it's still early, go back to sleep.'

'Hmm?'

'Shhh.'

Clint Eastwood's silent, waiting to see if she wakes up or not. I cover her with the duvet again and we watch her doze off again and start gently snoring her way back to the land of nod.

'I know who you are, you know,' I say in a whispery voice.

'Oh you know who I am, do you?' he says, whispering back as aggressively as he can. 'D'yeh think I give a fuck? I know yeh too fuckin scared to tell anyone anything about any of it, I know that. It's my shop, it's my money and I'm not havin grubby little halfwits like you running off with it.'

He's Hughie Jones. He's Hughie Jones of Hughie Jones Turf Accountants fame.

'I don't *have* the money any more, how many more times do I have to tell you people. I gave it to Harry my boss. I said for him to pass it on to whoever it belongs to.' I thought it belonged to Charlie Strange but Hughie Jones obviously thinks different and he's the one with the gun and key to my house so I'm not gonna argue.

'Listen,' he squeaks in his high-pitched voice. 'I've not got time to stand here and talk -'

'I gave it to Harry. It was all shoved up inside a Paddington teddy bear. I explained it, perhaps I didn't explain it well enough for him to understand.'

'I've heard all that crap this evening,' he says, getting loud enough to wake up anyone who isn't pissed out of their mind. 'Yeh gave him a teddy bear that was taped up. Told him to look inside. Inside there's a pair of bloody pyjamas. Yeh can't get away with that sort of crap y'know. D'you want me ta show you how fuckin serious I am? D'you want me ta shoot you in the leg?' He points the gun, he's ready to fire.

'No, no. Quick, please, no. I'll get it. I know where the money is. Don't shoot anyone.'

'Shoot what?' asks Sheena, rubbing her eyes and

looking round at me, at the masked invader with the gun pointing at my legs. She screams.

'Shut her the fuck up,' he shouts at me. 'Or I'll fuckin shoot her first.'

'What's happenin? What's goin on?' This is all Sheena's anxieties and worries about today's robbery come to life.

I hug her and put my hand over her mouth, trying to shush her. 'It's okay. I can deal with it. He's a friend of mine.'

'He's a friend of yours!' she shouts. 'He's got a gun!'

'I know, I know, it's okay. He's just on his way back from a fancy dress party.'

'*What?*' she doesn't get it. It's not completely convincing I have to admit. She pulls the duvet around her to cover up and give her some sense of protection. 'I don't want this to happen,' she says. 'This isn't funny.'

'This is my friend,' I tell her. 'It's okay.'

'What's he doin?'

'He's an actor. He's a Clint Eastwood look-a-like researching a role. He does a... this weird strip-show, circus act, mystery man act. He eats fire and looks like Clint Eastwood.'

'Oh shut up and get my money,' he says. 'Or I'll fuckin make your day alright.'

'Don't worry,' I tell Sheena hopelessly, which must be one of the most stupid things I have ever told anyone to do. What else is she gonna do? Not worry? She says nothing, I walk towards the door.

'Where d'yeh think you're goin?' he asks me.

'To get the money?' I've got an idea, it's a daft

stupid idea, but then my Mum's a stupid daft woman sometimes.

'Where is it?' he wants to know.

'It's only downstairs.'

'You get it, I'll wait here with her,' he points the gun at Sheena. 'So we know you're not gonna be doin anythin silly.' I nod and head down the stairs.

Mum. The money. Paddington Bear with a pair of winceyette pyjamas stowed inside his gizzard. Mum calling me a prostitute and a drug dealer.

Nineteen

Mum calling me a croupier and a taxi driver. I assumed that was just run-of-the-mill abuse, motiveless nastiness and lack of trust on her part. She explains things as badly as I do. We've got so much in common. I knock on the door to Sheena's room, knock again, louder, so she'll be bound to hear.

'Who is it?' she asks, her voice croaky and half-asleep.

'It's only me.'

'What is it?'

'Could I have a little speak with you?'

I hear her shuffling into her slippers and banging into the bedside table. A light goes on and she comes to the door.

'What is it, hon? D'you have any idea of the time?'

'I know, Mum, I know. It won't take a minute. It's about that money. The money inside Paddington?'

'Ooh, that,' her expression changes like she's suddenly awake again. 'Me and your Dad were talking about that all evening, we didn't know what to do with it.'

'Mum, what did you do with it?'

'That's what I'm trying to tell you. And first off, hon, I am sincerely apologising for taking something out of your room, I know I've crossed the line there –'

'Mum. The money, where is it? I need it.'

'As I was trying to say before you went rushing out earlier. We, me and your Dad, we'll support you whatever you do. If you're in trouble –'

'Mum. Here's the truth. I don't like banks, okay?

So I've been saving up.'

'*Saving? All that?*'

'Yeah, but I'm good, aren't I? I hardly ever spend any money.'

'You've done very well.' Mum smiles and I feel like I've made my Mum happy and proud for once. And I suppose the word for that is *ironic*, but in the list of words that come to mind, *ironic*, is queuing up way behind stupid, devious, hateful and pathetic.

'I was saving it up to go and study in Honolulu, Hawaii. Marine Biology. I want to be a marine biologist, that's what I've decided. I want to learn more about fish and apparently that's where you can do the best courses.'

'Oh, that's fantastic, I'll wake up your Dad, he will be pleased.' Mum gives me a big generous hug. She has to put her finger under her glasses to wipe away a tear.

'No, no, I'd rather tell him myself in the morning. The thing is, I need the money now. *Right now*, if you could just hand it over that'd be great.'

'Now?' Mum's puzzled. Like everyone else these days, she hasn't got a clue what I'm going on about.

'A friend, or well, not a friend, someone I know, was going on the course but he's had to drop out at the last moment for some reason,' that I can't think of right now. 'So he's got this spare ticket and scuba diving equipment he doesn't want. So I want to buy it off him. Only he wants the money right now, because he's emigrating... to Wales.'

'*Wales?*

'New South Wales, Australia.' See, even at this time of night I'm quicker and sharper than a swordfish.

'He's doing something there, a job to do with dolphins.'
Oh, I just can't help myself; I'm having to fight like crazy just to keep my lies alive.

'You can't have the money now. That's what I wanted to tell you.'

'What? Mum, I need it. I'm not joking, I bloody need it now!' I'm trying not to show my desperation, but I am desperate. I've got every right to be bloody desperate. I'm here, I'm thinking, Mum, do you want me to just tell you the truth – is that what you want? – because I don't think it is.

'As I was trying to tell you, me and your Dad were thinking about this issue and with all the breaking-in and bad people round here we decided to …'

'Mum, what?'

'It was in your own interests.'

'What? Where *is* the *money*, Mum?'

'We took it to the bank.'

'Mum no, please God, no.'

'What's wrong with that? We didn't want it lying around, like I said, what with all these robbers about. And they're very good these days, banks. I don't know what you're so worried about, hon. It's in this lovely high-interest account. Your Dad, he popped it straight in the cash machine, so there was no messing about. Safe as houses, though a darn sight safer than the houses round here.'

'Mum, can we go and get the money out, *right now.*'

'Well that's the thing. No, we can't. And it's not just because I don't want you to be too hasty with your spending, hon. I know that's none of our business, what you do with your life, what you do with your money, whatever.'

'Mum, what's going on? Could you tell me, please?'

'I wanted to tell you straight away. We wanted to have a conversation but then you went running off. It left us in a quandary. All this money we had to look after. And really, you'd be silly to just leave it in a bag or hide it under the mattress. Me and your Dad decided the only option we had was to take it to the bank.'

She goes on, she's expecting me to be pleased.

'It's in our account for the minute but we were thinking we should get you your own account set up – if you haven't already got one. It'll be easy to transfer across then – especially if it's the same bank. Come on, Hon, there's no need to look at me like that.'

Like someone recently drained of blood by a passing vampire.

'It's not like we're stealing it,' she says with an eerie middle-of-the-night cheeriness. Ho ho. Except I've stopped ho ho-ing some hours earlier. There is no longer any laughter in my life.

'Mum, I know you weren't trying to steal my money. Mum, *quick!*' My patience is snapping. I have to give the money to Hughie Jones. I have to give it to him right now or start learning how to dodge bullets. 'I need the money *right now!*'

Dad's hoisted himself out of bed and wheeled himself round to the doorway, and he's been listening. 'We'd give it you if we could,' he says, 'but it takes seven days to make a cash withdrawal from an account like that. You have to give them notice. And that's seven *working* days. The money hasn't even officially gone in yet. No, listen, I'll tell you what I'll do, if it really is an emergency, I'll write you a cheque for your friend, a post-dated one. How's about that?'

'Dad, Mum, why don't we just forget it, forget it. It's useless.' I start trudging back upstairs. I'm full of bright ideas. How much can a bullet hurt? They're not that big are they? I stop three steps up and just start crying.

'Hey, honeybunch, don't fret,' Mum's hugging me again, but I'm not looking at her, I don't want her to see how desperate I am. 'Your Dad'll write a cheque, just you wait here.'

I'm waiting here, then I'm going upstairs to hand today's ski-masked armed robber his cheque.

Dad's back in Sheena's room, doing the signature thing, Mum comes back into the hall.

'Who shall I get him to make it out to?' she asks me.

'Cash,' I say. 'Or leave it blank, it doesn't matter.'

So here I am walking up the final flight of stairs to my room. Mum's in the kitchen making a pot of tea, Dad's wheeling about in his chair, struggling with the doors. It seems his new sports chair isn't as sleek as he thought it was. But then it's got his fat arse in it so it can't be too skinny. He's looking for eggs and beans and whatever else he can find for the big family fry-up he's planning. I told him it was the middle of the night but he said it wouldn't do anyone any harm to get up a bit earlier once in a while. He used to work nights, Dad did, so he knows all about being awake at strange times of day.

219

I push my bedroom door open and switch on the light.

'Where the bloody hell have you been?' Hughie Jones asks me, turning round to point the gun at me, the sports bag he had over his shoulder resting on the end of the bed, ready to be filled with some heavy duty noteage. Sheena's got her t-shirt on but she's still huddled under the duvet like a frightened mouse.

'Gettin your money,' I say walking over and holding out the cheque.

'What's that?'

'Your money. It's what I owe you.'

He takes the cheque and looks at it,

'This isn't my bloody money. I want the cash. Do you want me to shoot you?' He's angry and shouting.

I shout back, 'Oh shoot me then, what do I care? It's in the bloody wardrobe, that's where it is. I've hidden it in the duvet, what d'you want me to say?'

Hughie Jones looks at me like he's thinking about what I've just said. He turns round and looks at Sheena and the duvet, then he looks at the wardrobe over by the window.

'There? It's in there?'

'Yeah, all of it and an extra fifty quid but you can have that seeing as how you've worked so hard to *earn* it!'

He goes over and tries to work out how to open the lock on the wardrobe. He should know how it opens; it's not like he hasn't ransacked this room before. He shakes it then gives up, turns back to ask me, 'Well, where is it, the duvet or the wardrobe?'

'The duvet,' I say, going over and pulling it off

the bed, off Sheena in her t-shirt with no knickers. 'Here,' I say, slinging it over to him.

He picks it up gingerly, starts checking it. 'I can't bloody well feel any money in here.'

'That's because it's hidden,' I shout back at him. I can hear Mum shouting my name up the stairs, she's telling me she's made me a drink and do I want her to bring it up or am I going to have it down there with them. 'It's hidden in the fuckin wardrobe,' I tell him. 'Right in there, right at the bottom.'

He drops the duvet, and turns round to have another go at the wardrobe, his back to us. 'Y'know I'm gonna kill you in a minute, I really am.' He struggles with the door, 'I can't get this *bloody* thing open,' he says in his singsong pissed off way.

'Can we have the duvet back?' I ask, going over to where he's slung it. I look at Sheena kneeling on the bed, my eyes saying more than a thousand words.

'If you help me get this bloody door open, you can have what you bloody like.'

The thing is, one reason why my room is so unusually tidy, why there isn't this, that and assorted bric-a-brac littered everywhere: clothes, books, magazines, plastic objects, broken electrical items, fruit bowls and fish accessories. The thing is, the reason why my room is so unusually tidy is that I've crammed everything into my big dark wood wardrobe. All delicately perched on shelves and in piles. Then there's the laundry, the ever growing, still needs doing, enormous pile of laundry. The laundry that always comes plonking out when you just open the door. So when you rock the wardrobe, bang the door, fiddle with the lock, kick and swear at it, when you finally open the wardrobe door, what happens is pretty inevitable.

'I've brought your tea up,' says Mum, coming in just at the wrong moment. 'Oh hi Sheena, didn't expect to see you awake at this hour.'

So when our masked invader finally pulls open the wardrobe door everything comes flying out. He steps backwards to get out of the way and that's when I jump him with the duvet.

'Quick, get him,' I shout. I crash into him, Sheena doesn't hesitate, she jumps off the bed like a monkey, filled with hate and rage at all this terror.

I can hear Mum screaming; I can hear Hughie Jones shouting. The duvet's over his head and we're clinging onto him like rats on a chicken bone.

Then something hits us and we topple over, the gun goes off with a crack and the window breaks with a tearing roar and a high-pitched scream. I don't know what's happened but I know I'm in pain. The duvet's over my head and someone's fallen out of the window and slapped down into the back garden.

'Mum,' I say, 'Mum, help me.'

Twenty

'Mum,' I say, 'Mum, help me. I can't peel this orange.'

'What is it now?'

'How am I supposed to eat this orange unless you peel it for me?' I whine. I'm getting very good at whining these days, I could do it for a living. I could be a whine tester; I could test if people are whiny enough. It's a thought, but it's not like I don't have enough time for thinking sad, useless, pathetically unfunny thoughts these days. Now that I'm not working.

The Hughie Jones chain of bookmakers is shut. The company has ceased to exist. Harry the boss has disappeared back to Ireland and taken Paddington with him. Charlie Strange... I don't know. I don't even know his real name. I still think about him.

Sheena and Axel. 'Which one would you rather spend the night with?' Sheena and Axel are driving up in the jeep on Friday, coming to pay me a visit. So then we'll have a house full of conversation and shared secrets. I'm staying at my Mum and Dad's. I watch daytime telly in bed, I moan about why they haven't got satellite or cable at least. I tell them it's boring round here. Mum goes out into the garden to tidy up and polish the trees, Dad goes into his den to phone up radio stations and complain. I thought all he did was listen and chunter under his breath, but he actually gets involved. He's making a career of complaining. He's even got his own website; he answers emails from other people that are complaining about things. He doesn't like the government, that's the main thing, he doesn't like any government, he doesn't like anyone official interfering in his life. He doesn't like broken paving stones either, but you don't want to get him into a conversation about paving stones. He'll quote you court cases, he'll tell you tales of people in America, email penpals he's got that have earned thousands from complaining.

So when he's not busy whinging online, I borrow his spare wheelchair and scoot down the ramp into his den and have a quick go at internetting myself. I go to www.askjeeves.com and ask the electronic butler annoying questions:

Why was I born?

What is the meaning of life?

Who is my mother?

Where is my father?

Why does no one love me?

And he tells me, Ask Jeeves knows the answers to these questions, 'Where can I find pictures of newborn babies? What is a scientologist? Where can I buy cheap maternity clothes? What is the best Father Christmas site? Where can I find the lyrics to Beatles songs?'

It's a great help, it's a great comfort to me is my new electronic friend.

Then I've got my police friends that keep coming up to visit. Good old Detectives Harper and Call-me-Jill. I tell them the same story every time they come and visit. Mum makes them tea and offers them a choice of cake, fudge or homemade biscuits. Dad tells me about my legal rights. He tells me stories about police corruption in America and the former Soviet Union.

'As far as I can work out,' I tell the police, 'he

seemed to think I knew something about the plan he had.'

'This is Hughie Jones we're talking about here?' Detective Harper asks me for the six trillionth time.

'That's right. As far as I can work out it was an insurance scam between him and Harry and they were going to split the money. I could tell something fishy was going on, that's why I decided to go and meet Harry in the pub that night.'

'The Hungry Squirrel public house, this is, just to confirm?' asks Detective Harper, swallowing his moustache with his bottom lip in that way he does. Detective Call-me-Jill compliments my Mum on her fudge and takes notes. Mum and Dad sit and listen, they listen every time I tell this story, we all know it off by heart, it's flawless, we believe it so completely.

'That's right, I think that's the name. So he came round to my house to try and scare me and I don't know, shoot me.' I laugh ha ha ha. It's an established fact that I laugh at this stage of the story. It was so traumatic, what else could I do. Mum grabs hold of my good hand and squeezes it. 'I'm sorry I can't be more help.'

'That's okay,' says Detective Jill.

I do call her Jill these days, when I ask her if she wants another cup of tea I say, Jill, would you like another drink? Then I tell Mum to put the kettle on. I'm aware that I'm exploiting my Mum's kind heart, but she does enjoy it. I'm not saying she wouldn't get fed up eventually, but I'm only here for a limited period. I'm like a special offer; she's got to get me while she can. I'm not staying here in the middle of nowhere for the rest of my life. I'm going to college in

September. Marine Biology, though hopefully there won't be any practical assignments in the first few months. What with my leg in plaster and recovering from a bullet wound to the hand. I got shot in the hand, but that doesn't explain how I managed to break my ankle when I fell over. I only fell about two foot. It's not like I fell three storeys into the back garden and landed with a smack of my head on all the old bricks and nettles. Then I'd have something to complain about.

Detective Jill tells me, 'So basically there *is* going to be an inquest.' I nod. I know they like me to nod, I'm very well trained, very well brought up. 'And we'd especially still like to speak to Harold O'Rourke. The Guardia are helping us with that one, so who knows. Anyway, it's been a very pleasant visit, yet again!' Jill smiles and stands up to go. I shake hands and say my goodbyes then Mum shows them to the door.

They think it was Hughie Jones who held up the shop in the first place. Charlie Strange is in the clear though I suspect he probably disappeared for good measure. Axel and Sheena know too much, but I know they're both good at keeping secrets. And Theo, Theo my baby little moonfaced brother is talking about getting married again. This time it's Felice he wants to marry. The only cloud on the horizon being Felice's insistence that she have her best friend as her chief bridesmaid. Theo says he can't quite deal with that. But they'll have all changed their minds by this time next week. Theo'll be on to blonde number seven hundred and sixty, Ava'll be stuck down the back of a comfy chair squealing for help, Felice'll have got a job as a builder's apprentice. It'll all make sense in some sort of nonsensical way.

Then there's the money. There's my career as a student to pay for but Dad says him and his compensation money'll pretty much pay for that. My big surprise was how easy it was to get into college these days. Seems if you can afford to do the course, answer some quick questions over the telephone, and briefly explain how you can't come down for the formal interview because you're recovering from a gangland shooting, they'll give you a place pretty much straightaway.

Besides Dad says I should spend all my hard-earned savings on something spectacular. He says he learnt the hard way that there's no point in saving for the future. He says you don't know if you'll be here tomorrow, you may as well enjoy yourself while you can. Me, him and Mum are going on holiday to Hawaii this Christmas. Dad's paying for most of it, my money's going towards the marine exploration course I'll be doing while I'm there. Very intensive it is, he tells me, lots of deep-sea diving. Apparently it's one of the best courses of its type in the world, or that's what it said on the website anyway. So I'm going to be seeing lots of fish. Close enough to touch, eye to eye with a trillion little finsters, trying not to scare them while I watch. A black-clad invader in a glass mask and hood, armed with a camera and an oxygen mask, swimming unnoticed through their silent world.

'Mum, I'm worried about my fish. I think they're probably hungry again.'

'What, those little devils? I gave them a big meal this morning. Didn't I? Didn't I give you a meal?' Mum talking to them even more stupidly than I do. She treats them like little puppies. I've decided to leave them here when I go to college. I don't want to have to be like some one-parent family, leaving all the crazy student parties early because I've got to get home and feed my swimmers. Besides, Mum loves them and they'll give her someone else to care about after I've disappeared off on my course. And I owe her something. More than just something. First she was nice enough to bring up my cup of tea when she could have left it downstairs and made me come down for it. Then she screamed and dropped the cup in fright when she saw me and Sheena wrestling with a man trapped in a duvet. Then she ran towards us, ran towards us like a crazed she-lion protecting her young. Slammed into the man in the duvet, knocked him off balance, he shot me in the hand and collapsed backwards and into and through the window.

The result is, my Mum'll do whatever I want because she feels guilty about getting me shot. I've tried to explain about the whole saving-my-life scenario but she won't hear of it. It's the getting me shot by being crazy and out of character and jumping at him like that. She worries about it constantly, makes herself feel better by doing whatever she can for me, spoiling me like I'm still her adopted little baby.

'Didn't I feed you, Kurty?' she says.

Axel brought them back from Harry's place. That was what he wanted to tell me. That was his big surprise. Apparently Theo and Charlie Strange went round there. Charlie went inside, kicked a few doors in, made a mess, threw some things in the air and punched some walls, then left with his usual angry look on his face. Meanwhile, baby brother was sitting outside all nervous and shaken waiting for Jeep Boy to arrive. When he did they decided they better check out Harry's flat, make sure there weren't any dead bodies lying around. Inside there was nothing except a pile of old newspapers, a bed with no sheets on and a soup pan full of water. Full of discombobulated little prisoners.

Harry was nowhere to be seen. I don't know what he had planned. I don't know what the fish thing was all about.

'Isn't that right, little Tanky?' *Tanky.* That's one of the conditions of Mum looking after my fish. Their names have had to be changed slightly. 'Shall we give you a few more flakeys? Who's the lucky fishies then?' They all crowd round waiting, even Baby Kurt seems to have bulked up a bit since he's moved here.

The door bell rings, Dad says he'll go.

'Come on little Lorraine. Come on little Kurty and Sally. Come on big fat Judy, there you go, you big bully, let the others have some. How's that? Eat up now, no being fussy, get it all down you.'

Dad says there's someone at the door wants to speak to me. Tell them to come in, I say. I never had many visitors when I lived in South Central, and apart from the police I don't get many up here. I hear the door slam shut and Dad comes wheeling back in with my visitor behind him. And for a moment my heart stops, then it starts again and I want to run and hide, but I'm not in any position to do anything but smile and say hello and pretend that he's a friend of mine.

Dad says he's going to check his email and Mum goes into the kitchen to put the kettle on.

Charlie Strange sits next to me on the sofa.

'I've been wanting to have a talk with you,' he says. 'I kept phoning but they told me you'd moved. ' He looks at me. 'I think I owe you a favour.' He looks at me with those eyes that make you wonder if he's an angel or a devil, and he reaches over to kiss me on the cheek.

Recent Crocus Fiction

Low Life, **Mike Duff**

Low Life delves into the criminal underbelly of Manchester. It's a comic look at the life of small time operators, petty thieves and credit card swindlers. If ever there was a novel to disprove the motto 'honour among thieves', then this is it.

'Rooftop Rafferty is no loveable rogue: he's into cheque-book fraud and would probably have your wallet and cards in the time it takes to read the back cover of this book. But despite a career as a one-man Manchester crime wave, he is an engaging character who nods knowingly towards Dickens.'

The Guardian

'Duff paints a picture of a life most of us couldn't even begin to imagine, let alone survive but he does it with humanity, humour and tremendous insight. What's more, he could teach a few vastly more experienced writers a thing or two about pace, narrative and dialogue.'

The Big Issue

ISBN 0-946745-91-9   £6.99

A Little Palace, **Janna Hoag**

A Little Palace is a comic fairy tale set in a fictional suburb of Manchester. It tells the story of control freak, Alb Wakes who bullies his wife and treats his three daughters like navvies. But when larger than life Tundra moves in next door, things begin to change. She and her drag queen son open up a Pandora's box of new horizons for the women. When Alb spies Tundra cavorting with the Norfax bank manager, he finally loses his grip.

'Janna Hoag's debut novel, like all the best bedtime stories manages to be funny and unsettling at the same time.'

Manchester Metro

'A delightfully funny and touching novel.'

Sherry Ashworth

ISBN 0-946745-96-X   £6.99

Looking for Trouble, Cath Staincliffe

The first in a series of Sal Kilkenny mysteries, *Looking for Trouble* was adapted for broadcast on Radio 4's Woman's Hour and short-listed for the Crime Writers Association John Creasey Award for the best first crime story.

'Struggling single mother Sal Kilkenny is compassionate, gutsy, bright enough to know when it's clever to be scared and tenacious as a Rottweiler. Cath Staincliffe's tour of the mean streets and leafy suburbs of Manchester reveals the city as the natural successor to Marlowe's Los Angeles. With a cast of characters drawn from the gutter to the high ranks of business and officialdom, she probes the city's underbelly in an exciting tale of corruption, exploitation and brutality. An impressive debut.'

Val McDermid

ISBN 0-946745-31-5   £5.99